Also by George Spain:

Delightful Suthun Madnesses XIII

My People: Stories of the South

Lost Cove

Come Sit with Me

The Last Giant

My People II: More Stories of the South

The Official One and Only KKK Hall of Fame Guidebook

JoJo's Christmas

Dreaming the Fire Away

SUNDANCING WITH CRAZY HORSE AND OTHER STORIES

by
GEORGE SPAIN

Ideas into Books: Westview®
Kingston Springs, Tennessee

Ideas into Books®
W E S T V I E W
P.O. Box 605
Kingston Springs, TN 37082
www.publishedbywestview.com

This book is a work of fiction. Names, characters, places and incidents either are products of the author's imagination or are used fictitiously. Any resemblance to actual events or locales or persons, living or dead, is entirely coincidental.

ISBN 978-1-62880-134-7

First edition, February 2018

Printed in the United States of America on acid free paper.

Dedicated to Jackie

And My Favorite Short Story Writers:
William Faulkner
A.E. Copphard
H. E. Bates

Introduction

"Yo know nobody eva ask me what it was like bein a slave an I's nevah said a thing till now...folks look at me an they's sees a kind-lookin, ole colahed preachah who likes to help people, an that's pretty much true now, but I hadn't always been this way. A long time ago, befo tha Lawd an Liza change me, I wants ta kill people, wants ta kill white peoples fo what tey done ta us...I'd wanted ta kill em all I's so full uv hate. Bein a slave is a bad thing, so bad you can't nevah know it, we wadn't mo than a bunch of two-legged animals worth lots uv money. When I wus fifteen I wus so big an strong I wus a prime field hand worth mo thwn a thousand dallahs... a thousand dallahs."

Reverend Billy Highfield, 1898

Table of Contents

Sun Dancing with Crazy Horse

Listen...

We did not ask you white people to come here. The Great Spirit gave us this country as our home. You had yours. We did not interfere with you. The Great Spirit gave us plenty of land to live on, and buffalo, deer, antelope, and other game. But you have come here and taken my land from me, you are killing off our game, so it is hard for us to live...We do not want your civilization! We would live as our fathers did, and their fathers before them...

One does not sell the earth on which the people walk.

Crazy Horse, Oglala

The wiwanyag wachipi (dance looking at the sun) is one of our greatest rites and was first held many, many winters after our people received the sacred pipe from the White Buffalo Cow Woman. It is held each year during the Moon of Fattening (June) or the Moon of Cherries Blackening (July), always at the time when the moon is full, for the growing and dying of the moon reminds us of our ignorance which comes and goes; but when the moon is full it is as if the eternal light of the Great Spirit were upon the whole world.

Black Elk, Oglala

We will carry each other around in our hearts forever.

Said to me by Wind Bird, a young Cherokee girl

Think you know a lot, well I'm about to tell you something you probably don't know a thing about but before I begin to tell this helluva tale about Indians and my family I want to give you a personal opinion: God never created any full-time saints or full-time sinners be they white, black, brown, yellow, polka-dotted, or red. While I've a lot of sympathy for my Cherokee ancestors and Indians in general I also believe sympathy alone can't overshadow the truth. Truth is: some Indians connived, lied, cheated, broke their promises, and massacred innocent women and children just like white people. Truth is: lots and lots of the first settlers who came from England, Scotland, Wales, Ireland, and Germany were poor as church mice and hungry for land and freedom and no heathen savages were going to keep them from cutting forests and killing deer and sinking their plows into the dark, rich loam of the land that they were convinced was theirs—since they were there, standing on it.

SUN DANCING AROUND THE SACRED TREE

Indians have been in my head since childhood and before that in my family's blood way, way back. My memories of them are broken bones and pottery scattered through my life like those I found as a boy when I put jawbones, teeth, and shards from uncovered stone-box graves into a cardboard box while bulldozers roared behind me and prisoners from the city jail laughed and cursed as they built new streets. I lost the box or it was stolen.

In October 1990, I was handcuffed and arrested with thirty Indians and others at Bells Bend, near Nashville. Plans were to turn this beautiful site filled with Indian graves in the curve of the Cumberland River into a landfill for the county. Indians from across the country came to oppose this. A line of us stood in front of the entrance to the site and prevented the owners from entering. They had the police with them. When we refused to disperse, we were arrested and taken to court, where the judge lectured us then released us. The plan to make Bells Bend a landfill was rescinded. It is now an 808 acre park used for environmental education and outdoor recreation.

Most everyone has heard of the Trail of Tears and the Cherokee terrible suffering. In the early 1800s, my people were removed from their land in Tennessee and Georgia across the Mississippi to what is now Oklahoma. Listen to their plea to General Winfield Scott in 1838.

We your prisoners wish to speak to you...we have been made prisoners by your men, but we do not fight against you...We do not want to see our wives and children die. We do not want to die ourselves and leave them widows and orphans...Sir, our hearts are very heavy...we ask that you do not send us down the river at this time of year. If you do we shall die, our wives will die, our children will die...if you send the whole nation, the whole nation will die.

Sixteen thousand five hundred were driven from their homes in Georgia and Tennessee. Four thousand, nearly one-fifth of the entire Cherokee nation, died on the way; they were buried beside the trail, and the living moved on. "Looks like maybe all be dead before we get to new Indian country," said one full blood.

This story is as true as I remember and as I want it to be. It begins with three tales my grandfather told me, when I was a boy, about: a hunter caught on the plains in a freezing snowstorm who killed, gutted, and crawled inside the cavity of his horse until the storm passed; wolves chasing a hunter carrying a dead deer over his shoulder as he ran through a forest toward his cabin until, just as they were about to catch him, he threw it off and escaped; and most lasting was of his grandfather's grandfather, Cherokee Chief James Vann, a leader of the upper villages who tried to save their lands and killed many people. He owned a hundred slaves and was the wealthiest Indian in America. He brought Moravian missionaries to live on his land, near him, to educate his people. He was a violent alcoholic and was assassinated in 1809. Here's a moment in his life—

June 6, 1805 Diary of the Moravian mission to the Cherokees. In question to [Brother Byan] the question [from James Vann] of whether he believed in Jesus, Vann answered, "No!"...he did not believe there was a Jesus Christ: all such things like that were imagined

On the 17th, Brother Wohlfahrt went to Mr. Vann to speak with him about his conduct up til now...it seemed as if harm and unhappiness stood before him. He then jumped out of bed, took the bottle, and drank in rage. He said that 'it was his house, and he could drink, dance, fornicate, and do whatever he wanted to in it; it was not anyone's business.

Now, at eighty, I look back and smile at these things and the mostly happy life I've lived and loved. Its been exciting and filled with adventure, fun, and laughter. Even when failures and calamities and regrets have come I've been helped by what I've learned from the mentally ill with whom I worked and by the love of my family and friends.

"Regrets, I've had a few," Sinatra sang. It is somewhat–maybe even a whole lot–funny, that my third biggest regret over eighty years, or maybe it's my fifth or sixth biggest, maybe even my seventeenth or beyond, happened the last week of June, 1990, at Medicine Man, Zack Bear Shield's Sun Dance Ceremony on the Wounded Knee Battlefield in South Dakota.

The previous winter Brad and Lynch, our first and second sons, collected a large truckload of winter clothing and food and Brad drove it to Pine Ridge Reservation in South Dakota for distribution. Not long after, Bear Shield invited Brad, his friend, Karen, and Jackie and me to come to the Sun Dance at Wounded Knee ...

The folds of the plains spread across the land like a rumpled blanket. Never-ending wind rippled the long buffalo grass as a woman's hair; blue stretched the sky from horizon to horizon. High above, a peregrine falcon circled making quick, sharp cries, suddenly, folding its wings, it stooped downward; just as it passed over, it turned its head toward us; and then, lifting upward on the rising waves of heat it disappeared.

Guards were at the entrance. They passed us through when Brad said his name. We followed the dirt road that wound its way through the long gray-green grass and black pine trees and there, on the other side, were tepees, tents and Indians everywhere on the gentle rise of the long slope and, a little ways beyond, were a level clearing and the dance grounds. But for the smoke of campfires the air was sweet as the grass and wide swaths of yellow sunflowers.

We set our two yellow tents up on a small spur at the edge of the encampment. Thank God Brad double stacked them.

We were strangers in a world we knew little about. With all our reading and education we were dumb as mud. In the days that followed they taught us with their patient kindness.

Custer was wiped out at the Little Big Horn on June 25, 1876. Four and a half years later and two years after Sitting Bull was killed, nearby, at Wounded Knee Creek, on December 28, 1890, the U.S. 7th Calvary surrounded some of Sitting Bull's people led by Chief Big Foot. The next morning, under a dark sky, someone fired a shot and the Calvary opened fire with rifles and Hotchkiss guns. By end of day they had killed: Big Foot, eighteen children, forty-four women and eighty-four men. Twenty-nine soldiers were killed. We visited the hill site where the Sioux were buried in a mass grave. A small white frame Episcopal Church now stands behind the grave.

Surrounding the dance ground was a large circular arbor covered in dark pine braches with an opening toward the east where the sun's rising would be framed. In the center of the grounds rose the sacred tree, a forty-foot tall cottonwood. From its upper branches four cloth banners—white, yellow, red, and black—waved out in the wind; ropes hung from high on the trunk, each one separated at its end into two lines that would be attached to strips of wood which would be pierced through the flesh above the dancer's pectoral muscles.

On the third day, before the second dance, Bear Shield sent one of his sons across the dance grounds to ask me if I wanted give a bit of my flesh to stick on the Sundance Tree as an "offering for the people." He was holding a scalpel. Jackie and I were sitting beneath the pine arbor. Around us were two hundred Oglala Sioux. Drums were beating, men chanting, women were making long, wavering, high-pitched ululations.

Inside me, my life-long-Church-of-Christ-ian self shook my head "No," not from fear of pain but from the stupid thought that if I didn't believe I would be "hypocritical." How sad. How very sad to have turned down his generous offer. To my eternal disgrace I don't have a scar on my shoulder.

But, and this is a wonder, he sent his son back with a long, wooden stemmed, red-bowl pipe. He leaned toward Jackie with the pipe held in both hands, "My father would like for you to pass this pipe around the circle for the people to breath in the sacred tobacco and blow the smoke in the four sacred directions. If it goes out here's a bag of tobacco and a box of matches."

Without hesitating she took it, stood, handed the pipe to me and I took a deep breath and blew smoke in the four directions, gave it back to her. She stepped backward onto the dance ground and slowly began to go around the circle, passing the pipe from one person to another, now and then stopping to put more tobacco in the bowl, relight it, then take a few deep draws before handing it to the next person. After a long while she finished.

That night I left the camp alone and walked a mile up to a higher field, sat down, and looked back toward the camp. The air was so clean the stars were close enough to scoop downward from the sky. Fires flickered, drums and songs rose up the slope; time went backward, yesterday was today...I was there alone on horseback, looking down; I was a mountain man, listening to the sounds of "wild Indians." I was the first white man there.

At night, two or three Indians would come to our fire, drink coffee and eat Goo Goos Jackie had brought. Three came almost every night: one, a handsome, gentle young man told us he had been coming to this Sun Dance for seven years to honor his mother on the "Spirit Road" to her resting place; the other two were friends since childhood, the largest, a broad-shouldered, bare-chested, dancer who wore a red-cloth skirt. He was mute. They sign-languaged.

The second night the dancer came alone. He squatted across the fire from me. I gave him a cup of coffee, Jackie handed him a Goo Goo. On the left side of his stomach was a deep scar where—like a parlor game making signs—the four of us began guessing. Finally someone said, "That's where your girl friend cut you." With a big smile he nodded.

Instantly, Jackie said, "George show him yours." I pulled my tee shirt up. For a long moment he stared at the eight-inch, dark scar and missing nipple on my right chest. He leaned forward, his face almost in the fire, then turned and looked at Jackie, his expression without emotion; then looked back at the scar and again at Jackie. You could almost see his mind conjuring up a terrible thought. He stared at the small, pretty woman who fed him Goo Goos—*She did that, she could kill you. How did he live?.*

We let him stew for a minute. Then Brad, in made up sign language, got him to understand I had had something inside cut out. Five years before I'd had surgery to remove a tumor. He looked at the scar again then nodded to me.

Above us, the drums were beating, the drummers singing; in the west, the horizon began to fill with all the lightning God had ever made.

We were in our sleeping bags when the storm struck. Wind jerked and pulled at the tent, rain and hail fell hard, water seeped through the seams to cover the floor, thunder-thunder-thunder and lightning cracked and flashed until we knew we might die and curled into each others arms to be burned into one solid crisp. Then it was gone and we were alive. Our tents stood.

Next morning the sky was clear. As I headed to the outhouse, I passed through the Indian's camp. Fallen tents were everywhere. Three Indians I had met were raising their tent out of the mud. I pointed to ours, "That looks bad for your side." They laughed, probably damning me under their breaths.

Funny works both ways. Ten minutes later as I was sitting on one of the three holes in the smelly outhouse concentrating on my business and the day ahead, I heard crunching foot falls and a voice say, "Hah!" Then, right outside the closed door, "Hah!" And the door opened and in walked a tall Indian, "Hi," he said and crossed his arms, leaned against the wall and asked, "Where are you from?" My business enterprise immediately shut down and I think I said something that ended with, "Hope you have a good day" and pulled my pants up and left.

Midday—a warm breeze—clear sky—the sun straight up—the tree's banners ripple eastward—the drums beat, the drummers sing. The flesh above the chests of five dancers are pierced, strips of wood inserted, ropes from the tree attached. The dancers stand with eagle bone whistles in their mouths. Four times they dance backwards—forwards—touching the tree—their feet pound the ground to the drums—blowing their whistles, stretching their hands and arms high toward the tree, then, dancing all the way back to the end of the ropes they lean backwards, their flesh offerings for the people stretching out as they push back hard with their heels, the old man's loose skin out three inches. They dance forward again then back; this time, at the end of the ropes, they jerk their bodies back and two tear loose as blood streams down from the bright red jagged slashes.

The women's unending cries rise above the throbbing drums and the high-pitched songs of the men. Everyone is standing; many praying and singing their language. Beside Jackie, the gentle young man, his face and hands raised to the tree, is praying loudly in three languages: English and Lakota and a third strange mixture of sounds, the sounds of glossolalia, the speech of tongues.

The three others tear loose and the dance begins to end. People drift away. Those who are not camping get in their cars and go home. The dancers return to their separate camping area. We walk down the slope with Indians to our tents; we hear low voices around us and laughter but mostly quietness.

The next day, more men are pierced; two pull buffalo skulls behind them over their shoulder-blades until they tear loose.

On the third morning, the drums and voices were low, almost silent. Everyone faced the opening to the east. A horse snorts. Suddenly, a handsome, long black haired young man rides in bareback on a prancing paint horse with hands, suns, hail, and lightning stripes painted red and black on its neck, shoulders, flanks and legs. He rides up to Bear Shield, slides off to the ground, lies down on his stomach and is pierced on his back. With the ropes attached he remounts. There was not a sound as he rode up to the tree and touched it. Then he turned the horse's head toward the east, gripped its mane with both hands, heeled its ribs and with a loud shout galloped toward the opening; as the rope stretched quickly to its end it lifted him up and his flesh tore and he disappeared through the opening. Then he was back, prancing his pony around the tree to the drums and singing and shouts of his people.

O my lord, after all these long years, as I sit here writing this I cannot capture it. How can a white man raised in the South as a Christian? How can I tell you their beliefs and sacrifices and pains as they have lived them all their generations? I can't capture with words on paper the grandness of all I saw and heard and felt. I cannot bring the Great Spirit to the reader as it was on that day and the other days. We were in a world filled with their long years of joys and sufferings.

The final day—the last day—in early afternoon a car drove up to the back of the arbor a little beyond us. A woman got out from the driver's side. She came around to the other side and opened the passenger door and helped an old, old man out. He stood there for a minute. Tall and straight, his long, grey hair hung down below his waist. His face chiseled from an Edward Curtis photograph made at the beginning of the 1900s. When those close by saw him they began coming forward to greet him as he walked under the arbor and sat down. His name was James Holy Eagle.

He was a hundred and three. He'd known Black Elk and men who had destroyed Custer. He was three years old when the battle of Wounded Knee occurred. Months after the Sundance, Jackie and Brad and Lynch visited with him and his daughter in Rapid City.

Then came the last day. Only one dancer was pierced and roped to the tree, with his upper body uncovered and his eagle whistle held firmly between his lips, he was magnificent. Powerful, tall, muscled–a warrior! He would have been hell on the back of a horse. At a dead gallop he could've knocked your head off with a war club.

People sat forward, their eyes fixed on him. The drum began, "bum, bum, bum, bum; the men's voices singing rhythmically with it, "hah, hah, hah, yah, yah, hah yah, hah yah," the women's voices began, rose higher and higher, "la,la,la,la,la,la,la,la,eeee,"

Blowing the whistle he danced quick, choppy steps toward the tree, touching it, then backward and backward until he was leaning his full weight against the tightly stretched ropes and skewers. His flesh stood out but did not tear loose. He danced forward again and again to touch the tree then backward to the end of the rope and still his flesh did not rip open–and then–and then–the fourth time–he leapt upward and backward–and his flesh tore–and he was loose.

Hokahey! It is a good day to die!

Several years later our second son, Lynch, his wife Sara and their two young daughters, Anna and Jesse, lived on the Reservation where he taught for four years at Wounded Knee School...

And a few years after that, Lynch helped Richard Jones at Lipscomb University, in Nashville, arrange for classes of students to go to Pine Ridge to work, which continued for ten years. Then, in 2009, I entered the following in a national Goo Goo contest. And so to the final story...

TAKING GOO GOOS TO THE SIOUX*

Twenty years ago my wife, our oldest son, Brad, his girlfriend, and I, spent a week camping with the Sioux on the Pine Ridge Sioux Reservation in South Dakota. Because Brad had taken a large truck filled with winter clothing as a gift to the Sioux, we were invited by Zack Bear Shield, a medicine man, to come to the Sun Dance—a traditional ceremony, where the dancers have their flesh pierced as a spiritual offering. The dance was held on part of the Wounded Knee Battlefield with guards a mile away at the road entrance to prevent anyone entering who had not been invited. Our two tents were set up near the circular dance grounds and next to the tents and teepees of over one hundred Sioux.

My wife, Jackie, a soft-voiced, Scarlett O'Hara-southern beauty, had an inspired idea of taking a case of Goo Goos with us. It was the first time the Sioux had eaten that perfect mixture of chocolate, caramel, marshmallow, and roasted peanuts. They were an instant hit! At rest periods during the day children would rush to our tent and push and shove on another to get one. But Jackie, who was as firm about good manners as she was beautiful, would stop them with, "Ya'll quit that now, be polite and ask, 'Can I have a Goo Goo pleeease?" When they did she would give them one. Later, we overheard some children mimicking her, "Ya'll, may I pleeease have a Goo Goo pleeease, Ya'll?"

At night, Indians would come and sit around our fire, drink coffee, eat Goo Goos and tell about their lives and about their ancestors on the "Spirit Road of stars in the sky."

Today, at Pine Ridge, I'm sure there are Indians who remember the pretty, soft-voiced lady from Tennessee who fed then the most delicious candy they had ever eaten and perhaps still say, "May I have a Goo Goo pleeease?"*

As I told you at the beginning you were going to hear a helluva tale. You've got to admit you just have. At one point I thought I'd call it *Scarlett O"Hara Among the Wild Injuns,* but that didn't seem quite right; it didn't seem to recognize the dignity and specialness of these people and of the other great tribes who have survived through massacres, starvation and, most devastating, the attempts made to destroy their beliefs and spiritual sustenance.

And they were not destroyed!

*This story won second place in the National Goo Goo Story Contest. I won a pile of Goo Goos. And may I add this, if Native Americans ever take back their country I hope they'll remember the Spains and take care of my people.

The Shrieking of Crows

The air moving through the open window was soft as a feather on Callie Whitehead's rawboned face when she woke that early autumn morning to the shrieking of crows in the woods beyond the garden and bit of pasture where the milk cow grazed

She was a tall and spare hill-woman "without a slice of pie anywhere on er," Grady liked to say. She'd only turned twenty-four the month before and had already had seven children—one a year save one—since marrying Grady Whitehead and leaving out that very day to cross over the mountains into Tennessee. She was with child again.

Over the years two of the children had died. "Tennessee," had been struck by lightning standing next to the fireplace stirring corn mush in an iron pot; a year later on, Nate died two days after being kicked in the head by their only plow mule who Grady would've shot if not for Callie stopping him from killing her, "She'uns ire eaten's maker...Grady, thairs times when you'uns dumber'n dirt...corn's ire life, without Kate we'd not made a crop an ire young'uns ud starve an likely we'd have ta cross back over tha mountains. But I'm tellin you'uns right now Grady Whitehead hell'ul freeze over a thousand times fer I'll do that...Put that gun back up thair on tha wall."

Grady nodded and put the gun back on the rack.

Long years later, after Callie had died, Grady would tell their grandchildren, "Yore grandma was some kind uv a woman. One minute she'uns could be tough as a plow blade an next she was soft as a woman can be. I can still see an hyar er as clear as you'uns...

'Lord amighty Grady, looka hyar at this yougun, hit's like lookin smack dab inta a mirrur. Saddie's me all over again, more'n any of tha othern. Look at them little ole blue bits of eyes, aire jus like mine, an her little ole nose an mouth they'uns mine too...My Lord, she'uns done suckled me out an's ready fer er daddy ta take er up...Hyar Grady, you uns getcha little baby girl an take er outside an show er tha stars.'

But that morning, when she'd heard the shrieking of the crows, Callie knew death was coming.

One Little Boy

Until you have lost your own little girl or boy and never found them, how can you ever know the suffering of losing a child who has touched your face with their fingers, and smiled at your smile and called you, "Mama...Daddy"?

Though it never leaves you, the sharp pain of seeing your dead child may dull with time. But, if your child is lost and never found and you're never certain they are dead, how 'then' can they ever be dead within your heart?

Over time, the meanderings of memories create new stories from the old ones.

June 14, 1969. Six-year-old Dennis Martin is lost in the Great Smoky Mountains National Park. This is a story of that little boy, and of a tracker who helped lead the search, and of the week I spent with him and two other trackers.

I cannot separate in my mind if what I remember is actually as it was or if I have created bits and pieces that are inaccurate since it occurred forty-six years ago. While letters, books, newspaper articles and websites have helped in telling this story it is possible some of my memories recall other truths not yet told.

The Mountains

At first the earth was flat and very soft and wet...[Then] the Great Buzzard, the father of all the buzzards we see now...flew all over the earth, low down near the ground, and it was still soft. When he reached the Cherokee country, he was very tired, and his wings began to flap and strike the ground, and whenever they struck the earth there was a valley, and when they turned up again there was a mountain. When the animals above saw this, they were afraid that the whole world would be mountains, so they called him back, but the Cherokee country remains full of mountains to this day.

James Mooney, *MYTHS OF THE CHEROKEE AND SACRED FORMULAS OF THE CHEROKEES*, 1992.

Spence Field, on the crest of Bote Mountain, is 4,920 feet high; a grassy bald covering 200 acres, herds of cattle and flocks of sheep grazed there in the 1800s. In the first week of July 1969, I lay in the oat grass in Spence Field, resting in the sun. Propped on their elbows, their radios on, J. R. Buchanan and Arthur and Grady Whitehead, Rangers and trackers for the National Park Service, lay nearby. We looked for circling buzzards that might lead us to the remains of a little boy named Dennis Martin.

In the distance, the Smokies rolled on and on like a graveyard of ancient giants. For a billion years they had formed and reformed. Then, 250 million years ago, ice and rain and wind began to steadily shape the flowing curves of the mountains we see today. Spence Field lies atop a stretch of the long Appalachian backbone that stretches 1,500 miles from Southeastern Canada to Central Alabama. Toward its southern end lies the land of the Cherokee, *Shaconage*, "the place of blue smoke," the Great Smoky Mountain National Park. Ranging between 3,000 and 6,600 feet high, the mountains spread outward over 522,419 acres, as far as the eye can see; their colors always changing: deep greens to black, variations of blues, some to deep purple; but in the farthest distance they fade away to ash and pearl-gray mists—then disappear.

The Boy

Dennis Lloyd Martin. He is handsome. Look at his photograph on the website—The Charley Project: Dennis Lloyd Martin. You see the smiling face of a little boy who might have been your son or grandson or one of your family. He is beautiful.

Vital Statistics at Time of Disappearance

Missing Since: June 14, 1969 from The Great Smoky Mountains National Park, Tennessee

Classification: Lost/Injured Missing

Date of Birth: June 20, 1962

Age: 6 years old

Height and Weight: 4'0—4'1, 55 pounds

Distinguishing Characteristics: Caucasian male. Dark brown hair, brown eyes. Dennis's hair is wavy and he has long, thick eyelashes. He was missing one of his upper front teeth at the time he disappeared.

Clothing/Jewelry Description: A red t-shirt, dark green hiking shorts, white socks and black low-cut oxford shoes with a simple heel.

Medical Conditions: Dennis had learning disabilities in 1969. At the time of his disappearance, his mental age was about half a year behind his chronological age.

**from the Porchlight international for the missing and unidentified website. Source information: Newspaper Archive of the National Search and Rescue School; WBIR News; Smoky Mountain Disappearances: True Stories from The Great Smoky Mountains by Juanitta Baldwin and Esther Grubb*

Disappearance

Friday, June 13, 1969, Dennis, with his father, his grandfather, his older brother, and two cousins, climbed the trail up Bote Mountain to Russell Field—a long way for a little boy with short legs. Here is the story as told by Ranger Dwight McCarter on the website of Porchlight International for the Missing and Unidentified–

The 1969 search for Dennis Martin is a tale with a beginning and a middle. Yet, the story still has no end [46] years later.

On Father's Day weekend in 1969, the men in the Martin family from Knoxville went on an annual hiking and camping trip in the Great Smoky Mountains. Six-year-old Dennis was just a few days shy of his seventh birthday when he made the trip with his father, grandfather, older brother, and another family who had a couple of young boys.

At around 4:30 in the afternoon on June 14, the group played in the grassy area of Spence Field along the Tennessee and North Carolina state line. The boys huddled up and planned a playful prank on the adults.

"The boys were going to sneak up and scare their family. The three older boys went one way and Dennis went the other way. The plan was for them to jump out of the woods on both sides and scare the adults. The older boys jumped out and everyone laughed and had a lot of fun. Then they asked where was Dennis. When it came time for Dennis to show up and scare the family Dennis never showed up."

At that point, official reports say it had only been between three to five minutes since the group last saw Dennis. Nonetheless, his father, Knoxville architect Bill Martin, wasted no time and immediately started searching for his son.

"They hollered for him, but couldn't find him. For anyone, it is very easy to get turned around in the thick rhododendron and rugged terrain up there. But especially a little boy," said McCarter. "Another problem at Spence Field is there seems to be an incessant wind that comes out of Tennessee and whips over the mountain. You could blow and whistle up there and the wind drowns it out."

Bill Martin hiked the paths in several directions searching for Dennis. The grandfather, Clyde Martin hiked down to Cades Cove and back. Park Rangers and other people in the park were notified and a search began.

As darkness started to fall, so did extremely heavy rain. It came in buckets at the worst possible time. The storm dumped an estimated 2.5 inches of rain on the mountain that night.

"The storm was so vicious, the people there at the shelter had trouble even lighting a fire. You have lightning and thunder and all that rain. You can imagine the people there in the shelter just imaging what the little boy was going through. That's all you could possibly be thinking. Where was he? Where could he be?

The following days the crews started searching the trails and swollen creeks for any sign of Dennis Martin. Special Forces were in the area performing exercises and were made available to assist the search. The search party now included the Green Berets with experience fighting and navigating the jungles of Vietnam...

**from the Porchlight international for the missing and unidentified website: (WBIR–Great Smoky Mountains)*

On June 20 the road to Cades Cove was closed as more than 400 volunteers took to the mountains. If he was found alive a helicopter was standing by to fly him to the Marine Corps Base on Alcoa Highway and from there an ambulance would take him to the University of Tennessee hospital.

The search and hoped-for rescue was getting national attention. Clairvoyant Jeane Dixon, who gained nationwide recognition for predicting the assassination of President John Kennedy, told the News Sentinel she "sensed" Martin was still alive. Seven days after he disappeared she told the paper "the boy was still breathing last night."

**from the Porchlight international for the missing and unidentified website: http://www.theleafchronicle.com/article/20...EWS01/903010346: Case of boy lost decades ago in Smokies still a mystery, by Bob Hodge, Knoxville News Sentinel, March 1, 2009*

[My response to the previous comment by Jeane Dixon is: such people are either delusional due to their own mental problems, or are religious fanatics, or worse, they are bloodsuckers who prey on mentally ill or emotionally disturbed people and their families who are devastated and praying for hope. For my part, except for those few who are mentally ill, the psychics of the earth should be buggy-whipped for their cruelty. I despise all the others for in my work in mental health I saw the damage they could do to people who were mentally ill, and to their families.]

"It went from hundreds of people to where you eventually had 1,400 people saturating the area. If you've got 1,400 people, they've stomped on everything. It just doesn't work. Every broken branch or 'piece of white' an experienced tracker looks for has been trampled. You've got search dogs that cannot sniff out any clues because there were 1,400 people there. We did searches back then like they were forest fires. You surrounded it and drowned it."

Any clues not washed away by the rain were drowned by the flood of good-hearted people trying their best to help.

**from the Porchlight international for the missing and unidentified website: (WBIR–Great Smoky Mountains)*

The search dragged on. People claiming to have psychic powers started sending messages to the Park and showing up to influence the search...

People across East Tennessee and the nation desperately searched for what happened to Dennis Martin. How could a young boy wearing a bright red shirt disappear so quickly? How could 1,400 people no find a single trace of him?

Theories ran rampant, but were mostly based on rumor or speculation. Some thought he may have been killed by a bear or wild boar. The shorelines of Fontana Lake were searched in case he washed away in the heavy rains. The family offered a reward for their son's return for fear the total disappearance meant Dennis was kidnapped...

After weeks went by, survival grew unlikely for Dennis if he was still in the Park. With the strong possibility of death in the air, that's where many searchers turned their attention. They searched the air for any decaying odors in the woods. They watched for vultures and buzzards circling overhead. The searchers found lots of small animals, a dog carcass, and a dead bobcat. Still, no sign of Dennis…

As for what happened to Dennis Martin, the question has no answer. The story has no end.

**from the Porchlight international for the missing and unidentified website: (WBIR–Great Smoky Mountains)*

The Tracker

J. R. Buchanan was ten years older than me. He stood five foot four and in his prime weighed 128 pounds. There wasn't an extra slice of pie anywhere on him. He was an ordinary looking man. But, everything else about him was way bigger and way smarter than most any man I've known! He once told me that, "J. R. stands for just plain J. R." Like his name, he spoke his thoughts straight, without twists or hidings. Tough as the mountains where he was born and where he would die he was a man who spoke truth, as he believed it. And yet, there was a great kindness and tenderness in him as you will see in his letters to me. He was good to me, and good to my family, most especially our son Brad who he trained to track.

The FBI nicknamed him "Walking Small." In WW II he served as a demolition technician under Gen. George S. Patton. In 1986 he went to Washington for the ceremonies where the Secretary of the Interior presented him with the Medal of Valor, the highest award the Department of the Interior gives.

On December 2, 2001 the Tennessean had a long article on him, in which he was called: "The bloodhound of the Smokies." As he sat in his living room during the interview he pointed to his walking cane that waited within easy reach near the door. It was made from North Carolina Bellwood. He spoke to the journalist in a raspy, slow voice. He pointed to his cane. Listen to his seventy-five year old voice—

"You can take that stick and whup the biggest bear there ever was...I done tracking. Some of them called me 'the bloodhound.' I tracked everything from the wild boar to ginseng diggers, poachers, pot growers and killers...

"It was a lot of pleasure to track down a person that was lost to bring them in alive...I enjoyed my work, except for the times I'd have to go tell somebody that their brother or sister or whoever it was, that you had found them dead. A lot of times, it was plane crashes or falls or drownings that would kill 'em. I believe I brought out and had to bring out 25 people—dead."...

**from the Porchlight international for the missing and unidentified website*

He learned the craft of following tracks from his grandpa and his great uncle when he was a teen-ager in the 1930s...

As a tracker, [he] was on call 24 hours a day. When he entered the woods, he always carried a gun, radio, daypack (with candy bars), flare gun, map and compass...But his eyes and ears were his most valuable assets.

"I've tracked all over this park...I never did get lost. I got turned around two or three times, but I'd just sit down. If you'll just sit down, start to thinking, then you can get up and get on, or I could have always backtracked myself.

"There's two things makes a good [tracker]. It takes somebody who has spent quite a bit of time in the mountains and a good deer hunter...

"As far as I am concerned, there have never been an expert. I still think that...The only thing I would say would be an expert would be a fellow who don't do nothing. You're gonna make a mistake. I still make mistakes and a lot of 'em. Especially up in the Smokies.

"You may be tracking a person and all at once, it may be two sets of tracks. You may take one of 'em and may wind up after a quarter of a mile find out it's a bear you're tracking...I've tracked a lot of bear...

**from the Porchlight international for the missing and unidentified website*

End of the trail

Buchanan and [Phyllis], his wife, live in the house they built in 1988...Cades Cove...as the crow flies is about four miles away.

He has a flower garden thriving in a one-acre patch of sunlight in the back yard. Blueberry bushes, 50-foot-tall cane, trees of every sort, pokeberry, Mexican sunflowers grow here. All types of wildlife—boars, bears, coyotes, snakes, birds and butterflies—pass through his yard.

Unless they do damage, he leaves them alone. J. R. Buchanan has a peace treaty worked out with nature, and after 75 years together, they get along just fine.

The Search

Jackie, my wife, and I had five children. The oldest was ten, the youngest a baby, our only daughter was six, the same age as Dennis. We lived in a remote, wooded, hilly and hollow part of Williamson County. I worked at a small mental health clinic in Columbia, Tennessee thirty miles south. I read every article written in the Tennessean and Banner about the search.

The intensive search ended on June 29, 1969. But, the very next day three Rangers were assigned to keep looking. I could not get out of my mind the horror Dennis' parents must have felt knowing the larger search had been called off and their son might still be out there. In his face in the newspaper, I saw the faces of our children. I think I was obsessed.

I decided to go look for him even if he was dead. Jackie said OK and the psychiatrist who directed our clinic said OK. So I went.

I am not certain I remember it exactly as it was but I believe most of what I remember is as is was—

On Saturday, July 5, 1969, I drove from Williamson County to Townsend, Tennessee in our powder blue, Volkswagen station wagon with a sleeping bag in the back, a kerosene lantern, a stove, some extra clothes, a backpack, canteen, a sack of food, and a couple of books.

I arrived in Townsend at dusk and found a small campground on the bank of the Little River. A restaurant was a few hundred feet away. It turned out to be a good location as every evening when I came back from a day of hard searching I was dirty and so my first thing was to bathe in the river, put on clean clothes and go to the restaurant for a good meal.

Early the next morning I drove into Cades Cove Visitor Center where I was directed to the Ranger Station. I was anxious and a little scared that they might reject me.

But low and behold the opposite occurred, the ranger, who greeted me, seemed genuinely appreciative of my coming. He filled in a form with information about me and told me to report the next morning at 7:45 A.M. and bring a backpack with my lunch and water.

On Monday, July 7, at 8:00 A.M. I arrived at the Ranger Station and was introduced to Rangers: J. R. Buchanan, Arthur Whitehead, and Grady Whitehead, three mountain men, one short, the other two tall, each dressed in neatly creased, mildly starched khakis. They had lean, raw-boned faces with intelligence and confidence in their eyes; men I came to admire and have affection for. They loved their world of mountains and valleys where they had been born and in which they would die. There was much kindness in their hearts.

And so, for the next five days, I met them every morning, climbed into a jeep and bounced up Bote Mountain on a narrow fire-road to Spence Field. What do I remember of those days? Disjointed bits and pieces—they may have been in different sequences, yet these I'll tell are photographed in my brain filled with obsession and some caution of danger—

It is the first day. We are spread out on a slight slope not far from the crest of the mountain. I can't see the others. We are crawling on our bellies beneath a "laurel hell." The entwined laurel branches inches above my head, are so thick they are impassable walking upright; the earth, inches beneath my face—initially firm—suddenly it becomes broken as though plowed by a sharp blade, the air is thick with the rank odor of animal. The next moment, immediately in front of me, though I cannot see them, I hear a herd of wild boar leaping to their feet, squealing, grunting, and crashing away through the laurel and a shout from someone below me, "*Hogs, don't move!*"

Another day comes. We are on a steep pitch of a mountainside, joggling and bouncing in a jeep up a narrow, rutted fire-road. Arthur is driving. Gears grind. The jeep jerks forward into a rut and tilts sideways downward. With every gripper on my body I grip everything I can, so as not to be pitched out, while behind me I am smothered by the sloshing, souring smell of corn-mash in an oil-drum, picked up earlier that morning from a still by J. R. We ground to a halt. J. R. and Grady jump out, lift the drum down to the ground, take its lid off, tip the drum sideways and walk down a narrow trail, spilling the thick-liquid mash onto the trail behind them and then I see, not far ahead of them a large cage trap. Arthur says, "George, tha hogs dearly love tha mash."

I am the first one up from the rest break and lead off on the narrow foot trail that twist along the side of a steep stone pitch walled by laurel. The others file close behind. It's the first time they've let me lead off. I don't want to do anything dumb, like tripping and falling off the side. We walk for fifteen minutes. My balance is good, my eyes and ears sharp. I am aware of everything. Just ahead there is a sharp, quick-cornered right turn around a stone pitch, with my right hand I brace myself and carefully step around the corner and there...six feet away...is a bear...the biggest bear God ever made. One quick sucking of air and I cannot breathe. I cannot speak. I cannot move. I am about to be eaten alive. Then, I suck in a lung full of air; I push backward. I push against a human being behind me who curses. I push hard again backward and there is another curse. And I hear what seems to be my voice whimper, "Bear." Sound and sight blur. Someone pushes from behind and I shove back hard. My eyes fix on the bear. It seems to have grown a hundred pounds larger and turned to me with its mouth stretched wide. Then, in a blur I see a leap of sheer blackness as it disappears from the trail and crashes downward into the wall of laurel as though it is made of tissue paper. And it is gone and there is laughter—but not from me.

We lie under the sun on the soft grass of Spence Field eating baloney and cheese sandwiches looking out onto a clear day and the far distance of the mountains. We are tired and happy. We've searched for three hours, now we are resting and eating and looking for circling buzzards—buzzards looking for the dead. The Rangers radios were on...suddenly, "There's a report of someone firing a gun from a car coming up Newfound Gap Road." We listen to the chatter as pursuit begins and a roadblock is set higher up. It is beautiful day, a breeze waves across the grass and as the sun shines on my face J. R., who tends to stammer and curse a bit when he is excited and there are no women and children around, says, "I hope they catch tha...tha...son-uv-a bitch on tha North Carolina side 'cause that Judge ul put his ass under tha...tha jail." Arthur stands up, hoists his pack onto his back, puts his radio on his belt and says, "OK, it's time to go." And we start down the slope into the forest and downward.

We are walking along a fire road, the ground is level, beneath the trees it is fairly open, we can see a fair way ahead of us. I am in the rear. J. R. and the Whiteheads are dressed in clean, pressed kakis. Walking behind them, I see how little they sweat, not a thimble-full of stain is between their shoulder blades or under their armpits; only a gnat or two flies around their faces. Their movements are easy as though they are walking from one room to another in their homes. At the same time, I look and feel like I have been dragged by mules through these mountains; drenched in sweat, swarmed by a million gnats, filthy and wandering in a world not my own. We come over a slight rise and see a little ways ahead a station wagon parked in the middle of the road. A bear is standing on its hind legs leaning into the driver's open widow. No one is in the car. The trackers shout, the bear jerks out and runs off into the forest. The car is Dennis Martin's fathers'. He is there searching. We do not see him. We move on.

The slope is steep and pummeled with boulders; a rivulet runs through the sharpest cut. I am careful. A fall here could break a leg or arm or worse. We go to a large "den tree" where a bear has had her cubs high up in a cavity. They show me the tree to teach me as they have tried to from the first. They love these mountains. I can tell they like me and want to share what they love. They try to teach me the signs of tracks. "George, look there, see them prints. You know what they are?" (I never know. As a mental health therapist I am pretty good at reading people. As a reader of animal tracks and signs I am dumb as mud.) "That's where a bar wus walkin' on its hind legs." And. "See them scrapings on that tree, that's where a bar was markin' its territory." And, leaning down Grady gently put two fingers around a small flower, "George, the deer dearly love these."

The next day, or was it the next, I left them and the Smokies. Forty-six years later, I cannot forget: J. R. and Arthur and Grady Whitehead. Rare it is in life to know people of such intelligence and wisdom and strength of body and goodness of mind. We shook hands as I left the Ranger

Station. They asked me to return to visit them and their families. Our friendship was born in tragedy.

As I drove away from the mountains and headed south toward home my mind went back to Dennis, the forest, the bears, the hogs, my new friends but then they began to gradually fade away and all I could think about was seeing and hugging and kissing Jackie and our children.

The Years After

After that year my family and I maintained contact with J. R. and his family. They came to stay with us for a few days at our home in Williamson County. We took them to the Ryman Auditorium to see the Grand Ole Opry where we saw Dolly Parton in one of her first, if not her first performance. And, we took our pop-up camper to Abram's Creek campground in the Smokies and fished and J. R. and the Whiteheads came and ate with us and told tall tales of their adventures with bears and boars and humans. One evening we went to the homes of Grady and J. R. in Happy Valley and shot our muzzle-loading pistols in their backyards.

For several years J. R. and I wrote to one another. I still have four of his letters to me and one brief one to Brad who took J. R.'s tracking course in 1985 for Park Rangers and the F. B. I.

J. R. wrote in pencil on lined notebook paper with his unique spelling, capitalizations and punctuation. His work as a Ranger is scattered throughout. He always concludes with words of affection. His first letter was written six months after my week with him in the mountains. It begins formally with, "Dear Mr. Spain." In all of the following letters he calls me, "George." The letters are given in full, exactly as structured, spelled and punctuated.

12—17—69
Dear Mr. Spain
I am sending you a Map you
may get to use it some day

[Two aerial photographs showing the area we searched were rolled up in a tube. I still have them.]

I sure would like to be back
up on the Mounting with you
again. We stayed on the Mounting
until Nov 25th and we Found nothing
but we got a lot of Hogs.
if you do get back down here
we may get to go back up on
the Mounting We have had a
good Fall but the hunters gave
us a hard time to I am off now
For 2.65 hours so I am goind to
Hunt and Fish sume Me and
Grady went Fishing to day We got
11 good Fish if you come Down
about June or July or Aug I may
get to Fishing with you.
Well Pall I hope that you and
Your Family has a good Xmas
And tell all the Kids Hello
For Me.
good night
With Love J. R. Buchanan

2-23-70
Hello George
I was glad to here From
you.
but sorry to here that you
all had the Flu I hope that
you all are over the Flu by
now.
We are all ok I am about
wore out. I sure would have Liked
to have had you with me I
had to walk in the Snow
up to my Belt day after day
and I sure got Cold we
had 2 Choppers but they had
to stay on the ground a Lot
of the time but it is over
now and I am glade.

[He is telling about a February 1970 search for Geoff Hogue, a Boy Scout who wandered away from his Troop and was found eleven days later frozen to death.]

Well old Boy you said that you
was goind to come down and
go fishing Well if you have
a camper or a Tent you can
Stay at Abrams Creek Camp
ground and I will be
glad to go fishing with
you and your Boys and I will take my Boy along

(page break)

he Likes to go with me
and we go out a lot
and when you get Ready to
Come Let me know and I

will be Ready I don't know
what days I will be off but
we can get to good days Fishing
in and Grady will have 2 days
so you can get 4 days Fishing
and the Best time is June
July and Aug but you can come any
Time and we will get in
Some good Fishing.
Well old Pal I am goind to
Stop For now I have go company
so I will stop.
Love J. R.

5—22—70
Hello George
and all.
And how are you all by now
Fine I hope.
Well as far as we are ok
I am sorry that I haven't
Wrote you sooner but I have
been working pretty hard and
I was on a fire this week
on the 20th and I got home
the next day I was on the Fire
241/2 and I sure was all in when
I got home and we got the
Fire out and I went back
On pt in the Cove to day and
In the Morning I will be
On the Creek and that is
My Last in the Rangers

Force for a while I will be
in the campground and it will
be 8 hours and I will be off.
and George I sure was glade
to get the Book I have n
my wife and Kids has

(page break)

I may get time to Read
In the Summer I have had
To haul 2 bears out of the
Campground one of them went
500. LPS. and one 300 LPS. and
the Big one we Shot for 500 LPS
and he went on he would go
a lot over 500—but we did not
get him but if he comes back
we will.
I have been Fishing some and
I have had good Luck
and if you get to come up
and Camp we will go and
have a time I am off
Thursday and Friday and we will
Stay all night i(you wanl
to. I don't guess you can
make this out but I am almost
a sleep and I have got to
be in the Cove by 6 AM.
I will stop for now so
Write me Soon
With Lone
J R.
Over DS
the wife and Kids said think

you for the Book and I think
you. So good Night.

2—4—72
Hi George and all.
I hope this will find you all ok
We are all ok I think I am Still
Frozen and I have been all day I
have been out all day in the snow
and ice and I had Plenty of
ice on the Parkway and sume
snow and We have got a lot
of snow on Smokey and I wish
that you and the Boys were here
We could Find Plenty Hogs they
are coming Down it is to cold
up on the Big Mounting I May
go out and see if I can Find
sume in the Morning.
I forgot to tell you that we are at
the Chilhowee Ranger Station now we have
been here For about 4 weeks I don't know
how Long I will be here I am goind
to Move over to Abrams Creek Ranger
Station I hope it may be 6 weeks or
more I don't yet but I hope soon
and we will be Looking for you
all to come Down and spend sume

(page break)

time with us and we can do sume
Fishing I helped the State Stock tuesday
We put 3700 [trout] in and this was one
More truck load come in and it

had about 3700 in it and they
Closed the Lake until March
15th so this will be a lot of trout
I chicked one man before the Lake
Closed he had (3) Rainbows—21½ 20 19 1/2
so when you come we will have a
Lot of Fun and I hope you will get
to come Down this summer and tell My
Buddy [our son Brad] that me and him will go hog
hunting he can carry my new gun
I have got a 22 Ruger Single (6) 22 or 22 mag
it sure is a good one.
I can walk for 3 or 4 weeks and I still
want get over half of my Dist.
We got 3 men For killing a doe deer
but they keep on hunting and we
keep on goind out after him I have got
(5) Bear Traps so they want use them
any more. Well I am goind to stop
For now so Let us hear from you all
soon and I hope to see you
all this summer at Abrams Creek
I have got sume papper work
to do so I will say good Night
With Love the Buchanans

The following letter was sent to Brad, who was twenty-six, after he had been certified as having, "Satisfactorily Completed The Visual Tracking School" for The F. B. I., National Park Rangers, and Rescue Workers directed by J. R. in the Smokies in the early summer of 1985.

6—3—85
Hi you all
and how are you all By now
ok I hope. Well as For us We are
all ok I have had a cold For
two weeks and I have still got it
and worked in the Rain about
all week I have been doing sume
work in Cades Cove on a case you
may have heard about it the Bones of
a Lady that was found I have been
working with the F. B. I. We do know
who she is But we don't know how she
died.
Well Brad I will stop For now
Write soon
J. R.

In August, 2000, J. R. wrote a last brief letter to me—

To one of my Best Friends
We walked in the Big Mounting
And the Little one and I
Loved Every day You are a good
Friend so stop By and we talk
About the good old times.
Love JR Buchanan

J. R, Buchanan
October 13, 1926–August 3, 2004
Visitation: August 6, 2004
Service: August 6, 2004

J. R. Buchanan—age 77 of Happy Valley passed away Tuesday August 3, 2004 at his home. He was a member of Happy Valley Missionary Baptist Church and was a retired Park Ranger from the Great Smoky Mountain National Park Service. He was a veteran serving in the U. S. Army serving during WWII...

Funeral services will be 8:00 p.m. Friday in McMammon-Ammons-Click Funeral Home Chapel with Rev. Steve Whitehead AND Rev. Beecher Whitehead officiating. Family and friends will meet 12:00 noon Saturday at Happy Valley Missionary Baptist Cemetery for the interment service...

On-line Memorial Program by Funeral Net

How could I not love this man?

What more can be said about the loss of Dennis Martin, the little boy lost in the Smokies in 1969 and never found? Was he killed and eaten by an animal? Was he abducted? Did he fall into a pit or wander so deep into a laurel thicket he was overlooked by the searchers?

There is no answer.

Why I am writing about him forty-six years later? It is simply this: he has never left me; J. R Buchanan has never left me; and, the Smokies, where I hiked the Appalachian Trail when I graduated from high school, and searched for Dennis for five days in 1969, and afterwards camped with my family; all these years and all these people have never left me. But, more than all these memories, the questions asked at the beginning have never left me—

Until you have lost your own little girl or boy and cannot find them, how can you ever know the fear and pain of losing a child who has touched your face with their fingers and smiled at your smile and called you, "Mama...Daddy?"

If your child is lost and never found and you are never certain they are dead, how can they ever be dead within your heart?

YA-NU

I know not how the truth may be
I tell the truth as 'twas told to me.

James Mooney

From 1887 to 1890, ethnologist James Mooney made several field trips to the Cherokee, gathering material he later published in a series of papers "relating to the history, archeology, geographic nomenclature, personal names, botany, medicine, arts, home life, religion, songs, ceremonies, and language of the tribe...[these writings are] the largest body of aboriginal American literature in existence. They were eventually gathered together into a single volume, *Myths of the Cherokee and Sacred Formulas of the Cherokees.* One myth told of Ya-nu Asga-ya, the Bear Man.

During the "Winter of Popping Trees" in 1786, a full-blood Cherokee boy was born in northern Georgia. As his mother looked into his eyes she saw goodness. She named him Astu.

Four years later, smallpox came among the Cherokee. It killed Astu's entire family, his father first, then his two brothers, finally his mother. The night she died her father, Yan-egwa, took Astu to his cabin.

Among his people, Yan-egwa was revered as a medicine man for his wisdom. Whites called him, "Big Bear." A member of the Paint Clan, he knew all things of life, birth, death and regeneration. He had kind brown eyes. He lived alone. His cabin stood beside a narrow river. Born with a second sight, he could see into the beyond.

The morning after his daughter's death, Yan-egwa woke Astu and said, "Come with me." He took his grandson's hand and led him down from the cabin into the river. He immersed Astu six times. Each time he lifted the boy up into the air and pointed him toward one of the six directions. Then he held him as high as he could reach above his head and said, "You are no longer Astu; you are now Ya-nu. Bear is your medicine. From this day on I will teach you the ways of healing and of seeing."

And so it came to be.

Many years passed. Then came a cold morning when Yan-egwa could barely rise from his bed. Now old and frail, he could feel his spirit beginning to slip from his body. When that day's darkness came and Ya-nu was deep in sleep, Yan-egwa covered himself with his bearskin so he might see into the beyond.

He saw Death sitting cross-legged by the river staring at him and whispering, "It is time...it is time." There was no sound as he rose from his bed; the air did not move as he left the cabin and walked through the grass toward the river. Death was standing and waiting for him with outstretched hands. He steadied Yan-egwa as they entered the water together. He washed his old friend's body one last time. Then they lay down side-by-side in the soft grass beside the river. And there, just as the sun was rising, Yan-egwa's spirit left him.

I was almost a man when Grandfather died. I could not stop the tears from my heart as I painted his face the white color of his clan and combed his iron-gray hair. I cried aloud as I lifted his shrunken body from the ground and cradled him in my arms. I carried him deep into the forest to the grove of sacred beeches. There, as he had told me to, I laid him on the ground beneath the trees and covered him with leaves.

Winter was near. The leaves were dry and brown; they crackled under my feet as I returned to the cabin. I gathered Grandfather's medicines together: the dried plants and roots in baskets, the powders and salves in clay jars, clothes, blankets, the bearskin, everything. It took many trips to carry it all to a cave Grandfather had taken me to years before. The cave was at the bottom of a high stone cliff. He said this was where the four-leggeds and the little people had come from when the world was created. The swimming things had come from the creek that flowed out of its mouth. The water ran downward to the river. It gave fresh life. I lived there for eight winters.

From the cave, it was a day's fast walk to Diamond Hill, the home and plantation of Chief James Vann. Grandfather had been his medicine man.

James Vann was a wealthy half-Scot, half-Cherokee alcoholic, feared by many and loved by few. He tortured and killed his enemies and thieves; no matter if they were Indians, Negroes or whites, he shot them, hung them and burned them alive. Though he could be unbelievably vicious, it was he, over the objection of other chiefs, who brought Moravian missionaries to the Cherokee. He knew that to survive, his people must learn the white man's language and ways. And yet it was he who, until he was killed, was one of the greatest protectors of the Cherokee lands.

After I covered Grandfather's body with leaves I took his place as James Vann's medicine man.

Every night, before sleep overtook me, my grandfather would come and talk to me and I would talk to him.

"Oh, Grandfather, it is you who saved me from the darkening land when I was a child. You fed me, clothed me. You immersed me in the waters. You gave me my name. You loved me. You taught me your wisdom. It was you who said. 'Ya-nu, one day you will become a Bear Man like me.' Oh, Grandfather, you are deep in my heart. I hear your voice telling of the bear who did not die, the bear who became a man." And, as I listen I become him, walking upright, walking on all fours, eating his food; the hair grows thick and long over my flesh. I hear him in your voice—I hear him speak:

A man was hunting in the mountains and came across a black bear, which he wounded with an arrow. The bear turned and started to run the other way, and the hunter followed, shooting one arrow after another into it without bringing it down. Now this was a medicine bear, and could talk and read the thoughts of people without their saying a word. At last, he stopped and pulled the arrows out of his side and gave them to the man, saying, "It is of no use for you to shoot me, for you cannot kill me. Come to my house and let us live together." The hunter thought to himself, "He may kill me," but the bear read his thoughts and said, "No, I won't hurt you." The man thought again, "How can I get anything to eat?" but the bear knew his thoughts, and said, "There shall be plenty to eat." So the hunter went with the bear.

They went on until they came to a hole in the side of the mountain, and the bear said, "This is where I live," and they went in. By this time the hunter was very hungry and was wondering how he could get something to eat. The other knew his thoughts, and sitting up on his hind legs, he rubbed his stomach with his forepaws and at once he had both paws full of chestnuts and rubbed again and his paws were full of blackberries, and he gave them to the man. He rubbed again and had his paws full of acorns, but the hunter said he was full and could not eat them, that he had eaten enough already.

The hunter lived in the cave with the bear all winter, until long hair like that of a bear began to grow all over his body and he began to act like a bear; but he still walked like a man. One day in early spring the bear said to him, "Your people down in the village are getting ready for a grand hunt in these mountains, and they will come to this cave and kill me and take my skin from me, but they will not hurt you and will take you home with them." The bear knew what the people were doing in the village just as he always knew what the man was thinking. Some days passed and the bear said again, "This is the day they will come to kill me. When they have killed me they will drag me outside the cave and take my clothes off and cut me to pieces. You must cover the blood with leaves, and when they are taking you away, look back after you have gone a piece and you will see something."

Soon they heard the hunters coming up the mountain and then the dogs found the cave and began to bark. The hunters looked inside and saw the bear and killed him with their arrows. Then they dragged him outside the cave and skinned the body and cut it in quarters to carry home. The dogs kept on barking until the hunters thought there must be another bear in the cave. They looked in again and saw the man at the farther end. At first, they thought it was another bear on account of his long hair, but they soon saw it was the hunter who had been lost the year before, so they went in and brought him out. Then each hunter took a load of the bear meat and they started home again, bringing the man and the skin with them. Before they left, the man piled leaves over the spot where they had cut up the bear, and when they had gone a little way he looked and saw the bear rise up out of the leaves, shake himself, and go back into the woods.

The sun stood straight up in the sky. The sky was as blue as the blue of a Jay. White light poured down onto Diamond Hill. Heat rose in waves from the ground. I was under the shade of a tree bleeding a slave's leg when Vann came around the corner of the house; with him were three or four Indians. He was drunk. He stumbled, cursed and kicked one man on the ankle. The color of his flesh—the color of a white man—flushed red with whiskey. I was kneeling on the ground with a flint knife, about to cut into the Negro's swollen leg when Vann tapped me lightly on the back with his riding crop, "Leave him...get up...I've got something to show you!"

I followed him up the slope and around the side of his house to a long log shed where he stored his trade skins. The logs had no chinking.

"Look inside! Tell me what you see."

I pressed against the shed wall, next to the door, and peered through an opening. Slats of light and dark spread across the inner walls and floor. At first there was nothing. Then, in the far corner, I saw a large still form. The rest of the room was empty. I cupped my hands on each side of my eyes and squinted to see the shape more clearly. I saw a mound of skins.

"You mean those skins?" I asked.

"Goddamn, boy, you can't see worth a damn, can you? Your grandfather would see it...he could even see things that weren't there."

The others were laughing at me; they were as drunk as Vann. One dropped down on his hands and knees, another jumped on his back and began to ride him around shouting and laughing, "Ya-nu–Ya-nu–Ya-nu!"

Vann whirled around and shouted, "Shut your damn mouths!" and struck them with the crop. He shoved me aside and threw the door open, whistled and called, "Bonnie Boy, come...Bonnie Boy, come!"

The others became silent. They moved away from the door and stood sideways as though preparing to run. I stepped back not knowing what to expect. Vann's face was aflame with anger and whiskey. Except for an almost imperceptible sound of shuffling in the shed, there was silence. No one moved. Everyone stared at the door. We waited.

For a moment there was nothing. Then the doorway filled with blackness and through it came the largest bear I had ever seen. Its glossy black coat glistened as it lumbered into the sunlight, its brown eyes blinking from the sudden brightness. When it was fully outside it stopped and began to turn its head back and forth; its snout held upward, sniffing the air, making heavy huffing sounds. It turned and fixed its eyes on Vann. They looked at one another, then Vann lifted his right arm into the air and said, "Up, Bonnie Boy."

The bear rose like a man onto its hind legs, its front legs extended before it, paws turned downward. It was taller than the tallest Indian. A white crescent blazed its chest. It walked toward Vann who began to chant:

He! In Rabbit place you were conceived–Yoho!
He! In Mulberry place you were conceived–Yoho!
He! In High place you were conceived–Yoho!
He! In Great swamp place you were conceived–Yoho!
And now, surely, we and the good black things, the best of all, shall see each other–Yoho!

When he finished, he took the bear's right paw in his hand and looked at me, "Ya-nu, when I am away you are to see to Bonnie Boy's care...let nothing happen to him that should not happen. Do you understand?" I nodded. Then, he ordered the bear back into the shed, closed the door and said, as he walked away, "Go back to your bleeding."

Five years before, Vann had killed the bear's mother while hunting. Inside a hollow log behind her body, he found her two-week old cub. He lifted it out by the scruff of its neck and held it squirming and squalling above his head. Turning in a circle, he showed it to the others whose knives had already commenced skinning and cutting up the mother. "This is my son, Bonnie Boy, in whom I am well pleased!" he shouted, mocking the missionaries whose Jesus stories he did not believe. He mounted his horse and with the cub held tightly across the front of his saddle, he rode to the cabin of an elderly slave couple who watched over a small herd of his cattle six miles from Diamond Hill. He left it with them to raise and train.

When the last of the bear's caretakers died, Bonnie Boy was brought to Diamond Hill. Trained to walk upright, to wave, to clap and blow a horn, he was a great showpiece for Vann to use to impress his many white visitors, and as further proof of his power to his followers and slaves. Within a year the bear's newness wore off.

Only when I made my weekly visit was he let out of the cage. I hated the cage. As the hate grew in me, I began to hate Vann. Except for me the only other contact the bear had was with the slave Vann had ordered to feed and water him. The man was terrified of the bear. He did his work quickly, silently. He never went inside the shed. He never spoke. He dumped the food and water through a wide opening between the logs into troughs and fled.

Bonnie Boy slowly began to waste away from lack of sunshine and exercise and, most of all, from not being touched or loved. His beauty and power were disappearing. His thick, gleaming fur was dry and dull; his muscles weakened–his movements slowed–his head lowered–his snout was barely above the ground.

When I unlocked and opened the cage door he shambled out and leaned against my legs, reaching out with one paw pulling me close to him, pressing his head upward for me to stroke him. He could barely stand. His head turned away when I tried to get him to do a trick.

We sat for long periods staring into one another's eyes: his small, round, brown eyes; mine, brown like his, only larger. At first, he would not fix on mine, but looked away. But then he began to stare back. And as he did, and as I stared into his, I was certain he was seeing my thoughts. And I realized I was seeing his. And then...and then...in my mind, I heard him speak my name and I saw–Yan-egwa, my grandfather.

Three months later, in the time of the ripening of the first corn, I set him free.

The Indians and most of the slaves were at Estanally for the Green Corn Dance. They would be gone for days, celebrating the harvest of our sacred food. And Vann was four-days' walk away trading for skins with the Creek. He would not return for weeks. And if he drank with them, as he always did, he would be gone a month.

I took Grandfather to the cave. I knew that we would be found and that I would be killed. But there was no fear in me. My grandfather had given me many years of life; he had loved me as I loved him. Now, I must give him life if only for a little while. Now, we were together again talking and eating chestnuts and blackberries and acorns. We sat on our haunches; he patting me and comforting me with words, "Ya-nu, do not be afraid, you will not die. You will live forever with me."

I had no awareness of time passing. We were there for days, I do not know how many. Then one evening, just outside the cave's entrance, there came the baying of hounds; the sound of splashing, the clacking of rocks and the voices of Chul-e-oa, No Fire, Kittichi and Falling—and they were on me. They beat me with clubs and dragged me from the cave. They tied my hands, put a lead-strap around Grandfather's neck and took us back to Diamond Hill. They locked Grandfather in the shed. They took me to the house and chained me to the wall in the cellar. As they climbed the steps to leave, Chul-e-oa said over his shoulder, "Chief Vann will deal with you when he returns."

Days, nights passed, but there was no awareness of them. There was no food, no water, no light, only black. All was silence but for broken bits of sound above me: muffled voices, laughter, a loud curse, chanting, once a gunshot, a scream, silence, more laughter, then the silence returned and did not leave.

I slept.

I do not know if I was dreaming or awake when there came the sound of shuffling in the dark.

"Grandfather?"

The shuffling stopped.

"Grandfather, are you there?"

"Grandfather?"

For a moment there was nothing...then before me was Grandfather's voice,

Hah! I rise from the earth!
Hah! I shake myself!
Hah! I walk upright before you!
Hah! I walk as a man!
Hah! I come for you!
Hah! You are my son!
Hah! Follow me into the woods!
Hah! We will live there forever!

The cellar door opened, a shaft of light slanted down the steps.

"It is time."

An Old Man

A summer evening.

The hot, dry air has not yet begun to cool.

The gray-blue sky is cloudless.

Across the sky, hundreds of buzzards glide on the rising heat waves, heading southward to their roosts in the pine mountains. Far below them, a man is sitting alone on a narrow ledge atop a red, sandstone mesa. He is an old man.

He is watching the sunset.

The mesa's steep cliffs rise high above a barren plain that stretches far away in every direction. To the west the plain ends in a dark range of mountains.

Just above the mountains the sun is a brilliant orange.

The man's eyes close as he begins praying silently and slowly—

Sun Father, hear my prayer.
My spirit is filled with pain.
Night Bird's small breath is gone.
She will not laugh again.
My people are almost gone.
Our sheep and horses have all died.
The corn and grass have no life.
Our land is dry and broken.
The rains do not come.
The springs have turned to sand.

Father, hear my prayer,
Send clouds filled with water.

He prays three times, then opens his eyes, raises his head, and looks at the sky. There are no clouds. The birds have gone. The sun is almost gone. All across the horizon the sky is bright red. He does not move. He is sitting cross-legged with his hands on his knees, his body is as still as the stone slab he sits upon. The stone is smooth and long. On the stone, beside him, is a small pile of feathers and painted bird's bones—on top of the pile lies a tiny stone bear.

The old man is small and shrunken by age and starvation. He wears a brown wool blanket and deerskin moccasins. His clothes are tattered and gray with dirt and ashes. His skin is dark as burnt corn. His black hair is streaked with gray and cut short in bangs above his deep-set eyes, it hangs in long, straight locks on the sides and back. A black head-cloth is tied around his head. The bones of his face are sharp; they are barely covered with skin. His skin is like parched earth covered with dust, every part lined and cracked a thousand times. The lips of his widespread mouth are white and split. It is an old face, weathered by sun and wind, worn and exhausted by hunger and lack of sleep—most of all by sadness. Now, only his son and one grandson remain alive. His wife and all the others of his family are dead. His thoughts are not clear. Since midday, what is and what has been have mixed together with things that have never been.

The sky turns deep blue. The same blue that was there when he first came here as a little boy on his father's back, holding tight around his father's neck as his father climbed the steep trail to the ledge.

He feels his father beside him, his hand touching his arm. He smells the sweet smell of burning sage and tobacco, the smell of his father who is leaning against him, whispering in his ear—

Look up.

He looks up at the sky. The air is so clean and clear, the night's first stars seem to almost touch his head, so near he could reach out and pull them from the dark. It is as it was long ago; his father's hand resting on his arm, his father's breath soft upon his cheek, his father's low, singsong voice telling again the old stories of their beginning—

Never forget all of this. All that you see around you was here before my grandfather's grandfathers, long before the ancient ones came, before the days of light, when Sky Father came down to Earth Mother. The stories I tell you are how all things came to be. Remember them, and when you are grown tell them to our people. Tell them these things:

When Sky Father came down to the great caves in the mountains, he entered Earth Mother and together they gave us all things that grow from the earth, all of the beings that breath. All these things came out of the caves: walking, crawling, flying, and those that swim came swimming in the narrow waters that came out onto the earth. And with all of these beings came those that walk two-legged, who became the first people; and as the two-leggeds came from the caves, they brought seeds of corn and beans and grass and nuts of every kind to grow in Earth Mother.

When all of this was done, Sky Father poured his waters on Earth Mother so that the seeds would fill with life and become green. But Sky Father saw that nothing could grow or find its way without light. So he reached deep into the earth and scooped fire into his hands and rolled it around and around until it became a ball which we call Sun Father. He placed it high up in the dark where it would give light, for the time we call day. Then he let it turn its face away for sleep and rest, for the time we call night.

Then Sky Father saw there were beings who flew and walked by night and needed small lights to find their way. So he reached again into the earth and took handfuls of burning coals and flung them across the darkness...

His father's voice fades away, the sweet odor and the touch of his hand are gone. The old man turns and looks to his side, then behind himself.

He is alone.

He looks down at his hands. In the brightness of the stars and the moon, he sees the veins and splotches, the twisted fingers, the long one missing from his left hand, the gnarled knuckles and wrists. He holds his hands up close to his face, turns them over, examines them, then places them palms down on his knees.

"Ha. Look my father; I have grown old. Soon, I will come to be with you. But first I must see my son. I do not know why he has not come. I will be quiet now and listen for him."

But he hears nothing. His lips part to shout but his mouth and throat have turned to dust and the words will not come out from his mind–

Where are you my son? My legs are weak. Come take me on your back from this place.

There is no answer to the voice that is in his mind.

The sun drops below the horizon. The last soft rays of light are red and orange and gold. The old man looks toward the far off mountains for a moment, then closes his eyes and prays—

You, my Fathers hear me! My people die.
Send your wind-blown clouds.
Send your gray-black clouds.
Send your tall clouds filled with water.
Bring them with their ladders of lightning.
Bring them with their roaring thunder.
Bring them with their many rivers of water.
Nourish Earth Mother with the life of living water.
Nourish the burned corn plants with your living water.
Nourish all your creatures with your living water.
Pour your living water on my people.
This I pray.

His head lowers. His eyes open and close. His shoulders slump. His breathing is shallow and jagged. He sleeps.

Night Bird comes to him, laughing, calling his name, reaching out.

He reaches toward her, then pulls back. His eyes open.

The ledge is shaking. Sounds come from the stones and the air beyond the ledge: growling, roaring, howling, ringing bells, and beating drums, growing nearer and louder until, from out of the darkness, shapes appear before him. They are real. He hears them. Sees them—

Tall shapes with turquoise eyes and twists of corn in their hair are dancing upright in the air; they are half human-half animal: bear, coyotes eagles, hawks, deer, badgers, antelope; they are crying, "Hu-ha Hu-ha Hu-ha" and chanting, "Ahahah Hi Hi Hiya Hiya Hiya." The heads of the birds clack their beaks; some carry plumed prayer sticks, others swing bull-roarers that roar like thunder, "nummmnummm nummnmmm," others are beating drums and rattling gourds and blowing eagle-bone whistles. Their painted faces and bodies gleam in the dark: coral, white, black, purple, vermillion, blue, bright green, and yellow; they shuffle forward, almost touching the ledge, grunting deep in their throats as they lift their knees high then stomp downward into the dark, twisting, turning, dipping back and forth. They jerk their heads from side to side, so near to him that he smells their animal smells and sees himself reflected in their eyes. He feels vibrations in the air, the dancer's movements, the heat from their bodies. They are gods, not men. They dance to help his people. He is strong again. He stands upright and steps forward into the air and joins them, half man-half wolf, black and red and white, dancing and howling over and over, shaking the war clubs that he holds in each hand. His lungs fill with air. His legs are swift and young. And then—

They are gone.

He sits alone on the ledge. Far out on the plains wolves and coyotes howl to one another. They begin their nightly hunt.

The air is cool.

A little way down the cliff, there is a clatter of rocks.

A child laughs.

The old man tries to stand but cannot. He cannot feel his feet and legs, or lift his hands. He wants to call a name but the thought leaves him. His head bends forward. His breath flows out without a sound. His lips and eyelids open slightly. Slowly his body leans sideways onto the stone slab.

The moon and stars light the ledge.

Just beneath it, there is a quick clatter of rocks.

No Country For The Fearful

The phone rang.

I picked it up.

"Hello."

"Chief Holdan here, one of yours says she's gonna blow up tha bank."

"What's her name?"

"Her nephew says she's Gayle Clements an that she comes to see ya'll."

"Which bank?"

"Southern Farmers."

"Where's she now?"

"Outside on tha sidewalk. Thev've locked all tha doors."

"We're comin."

Five minutes later, Nancy Page, one of our staff who knew Clements, went with me downtown. We drove past the bank. A medium sized woman was pacing back and forth on the sidewalk beside the bank. With quick, jerky, stiff-legged steps she looked up at the windows; the curtains were drawn tight, eyes peeked out between them.

It was 1978 in rural Tennessee. I was the third clinician hired for the new mental health clinic. I'd worked as a therapist at the Vanderbilt Child Psychiatric Hospital for eight years and before that part-time for two summers in the

Davidson County and Tennessee Psychiatric Hospitals in Nashville. I'd seen all kinds of mental illnesses. It had prepared me some for what was coming—but not entirely.

In those beginning years I had learned that people are not all good or all bad. Things had happened to them, bad genes, bad DNA, fetal injury; lots of things happen to us before we come out of the womb, and some right as we're coming out. Some of us cry our first cry out with good chemistry, some of us cry not so good, and then good things and bad things happen that bring to the surface the good and the bad.

In some ways it was the wild west; at times a barroom brawl. Four of us were serving eight counties, over 4,000 square miles, more than 200,000 people. We saw any and everyone who came through the door, sometimes out on the street, in jails, hospitals, where-ever they were: people: threatening to kill themselves or others, alcoholics, abusers of every sort, members of the KKK, people seeing and hearing and believing in things that weren't there, beastliers, schools with racial conflicts, delinquents, autistic children, and people caught in the briars of life. Slowly we grew and added more staff, then another county, a state prison.

It wasn't easy, at times it was hard, damn hard, at times scary—but I can assure you it was never boring, there were even times when it was fun. I loved it and got so much more back than I gave. I had failures, but one thing I'm proud of, no one I personally cared for committed suicide or hurt anyone. And our center became, if not the best, one of the best in Tennessee.

Well, let's get back to Ms. Clements. We left her pacing back and forth looking up at the bank and, here and there, I could see eyes staring out of a slither of an opening in the curtains. I drove past and pulled into the parking lot in the back and went in the back door of the police station that was a short distance away across the lot.

Chief Holdan was waiting inside, with her nervous nephew who told us she had tried to kill her husband the night before but had the wrong size shotgun shells. To his knowledge she had no gun with her now though he didn't know about knives or dynamite.

Immediately we made our plan. The Chief called the County Judge who agreed. I would approach Ms. Clements first, backed up by two officers with Nancy behind them. I would try to get her to go with me to the hospital voluntarily. But if she refused and became agitated and threatening the officers would come up and help me restrain her and then she would be taken by the officers to the hospital to see our psychiatrist to evaluate her for commitment.

And that's pretty much the way it happened. Except for one little glitch. I was only a few feet from her when she told me, "Go away" and whirled around toward the open door of her car where I could see a large open handbag. As she reached in I grabbed her from behind and the officers came up quickly and handcuffed her and took her in a patrol car to the hospital.

In the bag was a large pair of shears.

A Story of Two Wild Children: Wind Bird and Victor

What is written here is as it was, though some parts may be imagined; it is as true as memory can make it.

Scattered, fierce, and mute in earlier times,
Men wandered through the forests in all climes,
Clashing only with their fingernails for arms
They filled the woods with death cries and alarms,
The state of these our savage forebears in the wild,
We see before us in this young child.

Louise Racine

The wild child may have been a reassuring witness that, no matter how utterly a child is rejected by its parents, there is a benign nature that looks after all its children. The ubiquity and timelessness of such speculations cannot be doubted.

The Wild Boy of Aveyron, Harlan Lane

We will always carry each other around in our hearts forever.

Wind Bird

I have carried you in my heart all these fifty-plus years; even now, at seventy-nine, I see you standing in the open doorway of my office in your canary-yellow dress; your eyes and hair black as crow's wings, your skin dark honey. You say these words, turn away into the hallway and are gone—forever.

She was wild. Not feral. Not autistic. Not retarded. Wild. Unpredictable. Sometimes making animal sounds. She was short and strong, at times dangerous. Her mother, full blood Cherokee. Father unknown. She was eleven when she came all those hundreds of miles from Wears Valley, from the foothills of the Smokies, to the Children's Psychiatric Hospital, to Nashville.

Three days after her arrival, she leapt onto an attendant's back, grabbing him around his neck, pulling him backwards, twisting him to the floor, all the while grunting deep in her throat. The third week, she tripped a nurse with a broom handle, spraining her wrist. The fourth week she disappeared. The doors to the ward were locked. No one saw her run out. In an instant she had disappeared. Searching and looking and looking; she was not there.

And then, a tiny, mouse-like, eight-year-old boy, a tiny, fair-skinned boy, who had smothered his baby sister to death, pointed to a corner pillar, jutting out from the wall where a low wooden cabinet was built against the pillar. We got down on our knees, opened the cabinet door and saw an opening into the pillar. She was there just above us, just a bit inside the pillar,

She came out, kicking, scratching, and growling.

Born in freezing winter, the girl-baby came quickly out of her squatting mother onto a gunnysack that lay on the dirt floor of a tarpaper shack at the bottom of a steep-sided hollow. The mother tied a leather shoestring around the cord and cut the cord with a dull knife and laid the screeching baby on the cold, dirty gunnysack. The mother grimaced. She looked down at the wet, flailing baby, "I'll be damn, she's gotta lotta wind in er...I think I'm gonna call er, Wind."

An old man watched all of this with his watery, half-shut eyes. He was sitting in a ladder-back chair beside a tilted iron pot-bellied stove that was growing cold. He barely nodded through his blurred vision, then drank a long drink from the fruit jar always beside him; his eyelids flickered; his shoulders slumped to sleep.

"Goddamnit Daddy; hits freezing in yair, git up an git some wood an git tha far a-goin. I need ta heat up some water an clean that little un an myself." The old man didn't open his eyes or move. She picked up a piece of kindling, threw it and hit his knee. "You'uns go git some wood an build this far back up."

"Damn! That done hurt like hell!" He rubbed his knee for a moment then staggered to his feet and out the door. Even through the log wall he could hear the screeching of the baby.

Among the many men who came to her, Wind's mother had no idea who was the father; for they never seemed to stop coming down the steep, narrow footpath that led from the ridge road. Down and up the hill they came and went, Indians and whites and even an occasional black man; most brought money, some whiskey, a few came with chickens or a shoat.

And year after year, as she grew older, more and more, her mother would send Wind out of the house when the men came. But there were times, if the weather was bad, when she was kept inside. Then, she would curl herself into a ball under a filthy scrap of a blanket in the corner farthest from the only bed in the room. With her fingers in her ears she tried not to breathe, she was so frightened of her mother and the man. It was then she began to run away into her mind, disappearing into the woods, listening to the animals and birds panting and groaning and crying and calling to her.

While most of the men paid no attention to her, a few spoke kindly; but there was one who pulled the blanket off and began to fondle her until her mother broke a crock-jar on his back and threatened to cut his throat. Her grandfather did nothing but drink and sleep and stare into the fire until his daughter threw something at him. Then, he would stagger out and cut more wood or bring a bucket of water from the spring.

She was eight the first time she ran away into the woods and stayed gone for three days and nights until hunger and the cold drove her back to the cabin. But, as time went on, she ran away again and again. And, as she grew older, she stayed away longer and longer, eating wild plants, fruits, nuts, roots; sleeping in the hollows of trees; speaking to animals.

She told me these things. She drew them on paper. She made their sounds and drew pictures of the animals and of herself with them. Slowly, she taught me to understand.

I began to read about feral and wild children. Most especially, I was taken by a small book by Jean-Marc-Gaspard Itard, French physician and educator of the deaf. Published in 1801, his *An Historical Account of the Discovery and Education of a Savage Man, or of The First Developments of the Young Savage Caught in The Woods Near Aveyron, In The Year*

1798. Victor, the "Wild Boy of Aveyron," was brought to the National Institute for the Deaf in 1800. There he met Itard who affectively adopted Victor and began to attempt to teach him to speak and communicate with others and "to develop him physically and morally."

A child of eleven or twelve, who some years before had been seen completely naked in the Caune Woods seeking acorns and roots to eat, was met in the same place toward the end of September 1799 by three sportsmen who seized him as he was climbing into a tree to escape their pursuit. Conducted to a neighboring hamlet and confined to the care of a widow, he broke loose at the end of a week and gained the mountains, where he wandered during the most rigorous winter weather, draped rather than covered with a tattered shirt. At night he retired to solitary places but during the day he approached the neighborhood villages where of his own accord he entered an inhabited house…

Jean-Marc-Gaspard Itard

A small bit of me was as she was—Cherokee—my father's father: olive skinned, high, rounded cheekbones, great-great-grandson of James Vann, leader of the Upper Villages, hunter, whisky maker, lover of wild things; so my father. So am I.

I was drawn to her—to our shared blood.

She came all those many hundreds of miles from the mountains of East Tennessee to Nashville without family, without a friend, with only a social worker who did not know her, a woman whose eyes were scared, whose eyes said, 'I want to get this over with and go home', who, as soon as she put the records on my desk and signed the admission papers, fled without a glance or a word of goodbye to Wind.

As the door of the ward closed behind her there was nothing in Wind's eyes. I put my hand on her shoulder and she jerked away.

Wind Bird's records were in two tattered, gray folders; together, they were three inches thick. I opened the first one and began to read:

Referring Provider: Smoky Mountain Mental Health Center

Date: May 10, 1966

Patient: Wind Bird.

Age: 11.

Born: July 7, 1954.

Place of Birth: At home in: Wears Valley, Tennessee.

Parents:

Father: Unknown

Mother: Storm Bird, full blood Cherokee.

Education: Possibly, Grade 2.

Religion: Unknown.

Race: Cherokee.

Health History: Old scars are on her legs, arms and hands, otherwise no health problems. Though there are times she will not communicate her hearing, speech and vision are unimpaired. After removal from her home in March she was taken to the Sevier County Public Health Department for physical examination, at which time she received all immunizations.

Behavior History: From early childhood patient has had serious behavior problems in the home, school, and community. Becomes angry at the slightest provocation, during which she may scratch, bite, or strike others. She has destroyed eggs of setting hens, pulled blossoms from fruit trees, opened gates and let livestock out, poured the contents of slop-jars into cisterns, and prevented postmen from continuing their route by refusing to move from in front of their car. She has been dismissed from school five times for fighting classmates, teachers, and school bus drivers. When enraged, she makes guttural and screeching sounds like animals. But by far, the most potentially dangerous behaviors for herself are her frequent runaways into the forest, where bear, wild boar, and poisonous snakes abound. She may stay gone for several days and nights, twice for more than a week. During this time she lives off of wild plants, nuts, and fruits and vegetables she steals from gardens. At the time of her removal her mother no longer notified the authorities but allowed her to remain gone until she returned home.

Removal From Home: As result of complaints from school authorities and members of the community the patient was removed from her home by the Sevier County Public Welfare Department on March 1, 1966 and placed in a Child Detention Home. Subsequently, by order of Sevier County Juvenile Judge Jack Stanley, the Mental Health Center saw the patient twice: March 14 and April 12.

Evaluation: Though the patient was resistant to testing and interviewing she is in no way psychotic, intellectually limited, deaf, mute, or autistic. Rather, she appears to be highly observant and reactive to others in a manner that suggests her driving force is to avoid being controlled by others and, failing this, her aggressive impulses are to combat them and, that failing, to flee from them.

Due to the abuses she has experienced, it might well be surmised that beneath her aggressive behavior is a great amount of fear and need for security, acceptance, and affection.

It is our belief that this patient will benefit from a period of hospitalization followed by prolonged residential care during which time she should receive schooling and regular psychotherapy. Her mother is agreeable with this recommendation and does not oppose the Tennessee Department of Public Welfare having custody of her daughter.

Payment: Payment for the patient's hospitalization will be made by the Tennessee Department of Mental Illness and Mental Retardation.

[The boy was] a disgustingly dirty child affected with spasmodic movements, and often convulsions, who swayed back and forth ceaselessly like certain animals in a zoo, who bit and scratched those who opposed him, who showed no affection for those who took care of him; and who was, in short, indifferent to everything and attentive to nothing...

[Escape was his obsession,] when observed in his room...his eyes [turned] constantly toward the window, gazing sadly into space. If a stormy wind then chanced to blow, if the sun suddenly came from behind the clouds brilliantly illuminating the skies, he expressed an almost convulsive joy with clamorous peals of laughter, during which all his movements backward and forward very much resembled a kind of leap he would like to take, in order to break through the window and dash into the garden. Sometimes instead of these joyful emotions, he exhibited a kind of frantic rage, wrung his hands, pressed closed fists to his eyes, gnashed his teeth audibly, and became dangerous to those who were near him.

I was Wind's therapist. I saw her, twice a week in my office during the year she was in the hospital, and, afterwards, once a week during the three years she was in the Christian Children's Home in Nashville.

I was never afraid of her. She never attacked me. At the beginning, I was intellectually fascinated by her being Cherokee and by her past life and behavior; then, over time, I began to like her and, toward the end, we came to love one another. She was special.

At first, she did not want to come. But when she understood we would leave the ward, she came readily. I knew she saw this as a chance to escape. My hand stayed near her. She knew it, so she never lunged away. She said nothing. She walked beside me down the hallway and turned into my office. I closed the door behind us. So we began.

That first time, for twenty minutes or so, she roamed around the office carefully studying photographs and pictures on the walls, most especially the etchings of a Gyrfalcon and a Red-tailed Hawk. I could see her eyes fix on the hawk's eyes; slowly she raised her right arm, reached out with her fingers and gently stroked the hawk's head as she made faint, high-pitched sucking sounds between her closed lips. She turned and looked at me. There was no expression on her face. "I help hawks that have been hurt. I'm a falconer," I said.

She continued around the office, now and then picking up objects and smelling them, once putting a small bronze deer to her mouth and touching it with the tip of her tongue. From across my desk, she saw a green vase filled with hawk feathers. She could not reach the vase from her side so she came around until she was by my chair. She took three feathers out and rubbed them across her face, again making sucking sounds.

The office had a large window. The blinds were raised. It looked out into a manicured, grassed courtyard with two large oaks. The air was green with the sun's brightness. She stood in front of the window; for a long while she stared at the grass and trees and sky. And then, suddenly, she sprang upward onto the windowsill and began to pound with her fists on the glass panes, making little sounds and crying, "Please…Please…Please!" until I grabbed her around the waist and pulled her down. She growled, and kicked, and scratched, and cursed.

[These are my aims:]

1st To interest [the wild boy] in social life by rendering it more pleasant for him than the one he was then leading, and above all more like the life he had just left.

2nd To awaken his nervous sensibility by the most energetic stimulation, and occasionally by intense emotion.

3rd To extend the range of his ideas by giving him new needs and by increasing his social contacts.

4th To lead him to the use of speech by subjecting him to the necessity of imitation.

5th To make him exercise the simplest mental operations, first concerning objects of his physical needs, and later the objects of instruction.

All I sought at the first was her trust.

The next day, I gave her a Red Tail Hawk's tail feather.

She took it and turned away.

The next day she was waiting at the ward's door.

That day, in my office, she drew a picture filled with trees and birds and animals. They were highly detailed and realistic. Above them was something that resembled a face, part animal, part human. She would not tell me what it was or explain what it meant. She handed the picture to me. I thanked her. She said nothing. She made no sounds.

The next day, when I unlocked the door and stepped inside, she was hunkered down next to the wall; she looked up at me, straight into my eyes. Without a word she stood up and took my hand. When we entered my office she immediately saw her picture taped to the wall next to my desk. Her mouth opened slightly as though she was about to speak. But she did not. From that day on she was always waiting at the door when I came.

I learned from the head nurse that she loved fruits and nuts and raw eggs, so I began to have them in my office as treats. Slowly she began to make quick smiles and talk with me in her mountain language.

Then, three months along, I knew Wind trusted me as I trusted her. I began to take her out of the hospital onto the grounds. And it was that first day, as we went out into the courtyard, I saw her cry. Then she dried her eyes, looked straight into the sun and smiled and began to whistle like a quail.

As the months passed our walks lengthened, taking us beyond the courtyard to the larger campus with its wide yards, trimmed hedges, oaks, maples, magnolias, and elms. Whether a burning hot day or freezing cold, she had the habit, as we left the building, of stopping and raising her face to the sky with her mouth opened wide and flicking her tongue out to, "taste tha ire, fer hit feeds me." And then, she would run ahead: skipping, leaping, twirling, whistling, cawing, chirping, and now and then, when she came to her special maple with its low limbs, she would spring up onto its trunk and climb fast as a squirrel and scoot out onto a limb from where she would gesture for me to join her, laughing, "Mr. Spain, yer a big ole sissy."

How could I not love her?

[Once, in an attempt to teach Victor vowel sounds, Itard rapped Victor's fingers with a small stick when he erred in the task.]

I cannot describe how unhappy he looked with his eyes thus closed and with tears escaping from them every now and then. Oh! How ready I was on this occasion, as on many others, to give up my self-imposed task and regard as wasted the time I had already given to it! How many times did I regret ever having known this child, and freely condemn the sterile and inhuman curiosity of the men who first tore him from his innocent and happy life…

[And later, as his despair for Victor making any significant improvement increased, Itard wrote,]

Unhappy creature, I cried as if he could hear me, and with real anguish of heart…since my labors are wasted and yours' fruitless, take again the road to your forests and the taste for your primitive life. Or if your new needs make you depend on a society in which you have no place, go, expiate your misfortune, die of misery and boredom at Bicetre [the asylum]…

Wind lived in the hospital for a year. Gradually, outwardly, she became domesticated. Her outbursts of rage became fewer and fewer, her attacks on others stopped; she no longer attempted to flee. She began to read and write and sit at a desk, to use a knife and fork instead of her hands;

most special to me, she began to laugh at funny things and look sad when she heard something that was sad. Yet, she still did not participate in games and play with the other children. She showed little feeling toward adults other than me and a motherly nurse and a young, woman teacher, and often scowled at them when she was told to do something she did not like.

It was only when I received permission to take her and two other children—along with an aide—off the ward to a remote lake within a hilly forest that stretched for miles and miles that I saw that the wildness was still in her. For, as soon as we were out of the car, she ran ahead making her animal sounds and leapt into the lake and swam out, dipping under water, then springing up and shouting, "Come on…come on…come on!" And I did. And we did. And it was at that moment, as if she were my daughter.

When the severity of the season drove every other person out of the garden, he delighted in taking many turns around it; after which he used to seat himself on the edge of a basin of water. I have often stopped for whole hours together, and with unspeakable pleasure, to examine him in this situation; to observe as all of his convulsive motions, and that continual balancing of his whole body diminished, and by degrees subsided to give place to a more tranquil attitude and how insensibly his face, insignificant or distorted as it might be, took the well-defined character of sorrow, or melancholy reverie, in proportion as his eyes were steadily fixed on the surface of the water, and when he threw into it, from time to time, some remains of withered leaves. When in a moon-light, the rays of that luminary penetrated into his room he seldom failed to awake out of his sleep, and to place himself before the window. There he remained, during a part of the night, staring motionless, his neck extended, his eyes fixed towards the country illuminated by the moon, and, carried away in a sort of contemplative ecstasy, the silence of which was only interrupted by deep-drawn-inspirations, after considerable intervals, and which were always accompanied by a feeble and plaintive sound.

A few days after her twelfth birthday Wind was discharged to a Christian Children's Home in Nashville. I continued to see her twice a month for three years. With patience, love, and firmness, her house parents and teachers transformed her into a well spoken, courteous, and considerate person. And, with their help, she reached her appropriate grade level in school in two and a half years. How we celebrated! I gave her copies of the *Audubon Field Guide to the Southeastern States* and a collection of Wordsworth's poetry. Not only had she caught up in school but her pronunciation was, but for an occasional lapse, free of mountain dialect.

On July 7, 1970, Wind's fifteenth birthday, I received the phone call I knew would one day come. She was returning home. Her mother, Storm Bird, had reformed her own life. She was no longer a prostitute. She had stopped drinking and joined the Wears Valley Pentecostal Church. She had a full time job as a housekeeper at a resort hotel at the edge of the Park. She had moved into the small town and rented a house trailer. Her father was dead; she wanted her daughter back. After verifying the mother's stability to properly care for Wind, the Home's social worker was taking her home.

I saw her the last time on July 14, 1970. We held hands walking across the campus; neither of us spoke. She stopped before her favorite climbing tree, let go of my hand, walked over to the tree, reached around the trunk, pressed her cheek against it and hugged it.

We returned to my office where we both cried. Then the time came, she turned away into the hallway and was gone forever.

Later on, months later on, I attempted to contact her. I was not successful. I never heard from Wind again.

We will always carry each other around in our hearts forever.

Finally, however, seeing that the continuation of my efforts and the passing of time brought about no change, I resigned my efforts to the necessity of giving up any attempts to produce speech, and abandoned my pupil to incurable dumbness...I was obliged to restrain myself and once more to see with resignation [my] hopes, like so many others, vanish before an unforeseen obstacle.

In 1828, Victor died in the home of Madame Guerin, his caretaker. He was forty. Itard died ten years later.

Dear Wind,

Are you still alive? Did you marry? Did you have children? How are you? I pray that you are and that you are happy. You are still in my heart. Am I in yours?

Love, George Spain
January 2016

Codicil to My Will of May 1, 1861

To Benjamin Pearson Magruder, my beloved son "Ben," I am attaching this codicil to my will so you will understand that you are not to blame for any of the horrors that have come to our family. What I have done is for one purpose only—to protect you. I love you more than life itself. Know this from me: There is no demon in you; there is only goodness. May God bless you and keep you.

Be it known to all, what I write here of our family is true. I swear it on my mother's Bible, which lies before me, so help me God!

On June 10, 1865, in Maury County Tennessee, one month after the war ended, Ben discovered my father's body in the boxwood garden behind Father's house. The force of the pistol ball to his head had knocked him backward against the iron bench beneath an arbor of pink roses. The arbor stands at the far end of a long brick walkway sided by two rows of dark green boxwoods. Father's derringer lay on the ground beside him. Though he left no note, everyone assumed he had killed himself because of grief over the death of his sons—my brothers Robert and John—and because of the loss of all of his wealth, his hundreds of slaves, crops, cattle, sheep, hogs, and all of his money. All that was left were two houses, a few barns, three horses, and thousands of acres of untilled fields in Tennessee and Mississippi that were being steadily overgrown in weeds, briars and scrub pines.

My father, Benjamin Lucretius Magruder, was sixty-six when he died. He died on his birthday.

Though five months have passed since Ben found his grandfather's body, he still cries out in his sleep. Ben is only ten. He is my only child.

No one anticipated that my father would commit suicide. With our surrender he was openly bitter and worried about the future, but that was true of all of us. Mama told everyone she had not had the slightest worry about leaving him alone. That morning she had walked across the pike to our house to help Mary, my wife, prepare the dinner and cake for his birthday party. Our homes are four miles south of Columbia, on opposite sides of Pulaski Pike, his on the east side, mine on the west. Our entrances face one another. The houses are set back over two hundred yards from the pike. Together, the two places cover over three thousand acres of the best land in Maury County. He brought us here from Charleston in 1840. The houses are nearly identical: Georgian style, two-story red brick with plain fronts. Kitchens extend to the rear. The old slave quarters are a hundred yards behind the house, the barns beyond. Oaks, maples, tulip poplars shade the houses and lawns. Like the houses, the flower gardens are almost identical in design and planting. Now, uncared for, they, like the fields, are rapidly turning to weeds.

The morning of Father's birthday, I saddled my horse and told Mary I was going to Columbia on business but would be back in time to help her and Mama set up for the party. Since a few neighbors had been invited, Father was to be there by five o'clock to greet the guests.

He did not come. At five thirty, guests started arriving. Still he had not come. Everything was ready.

Mama was pacing back and forth in the front hall, ushering everyone into the front parlor to have a glass of dandelion wine. Then she would return to the front door to look down the long, narrow lane to the pike. I could see the wide look growing in her eyes, the look she got when she was starting to get upset. She began to rapidly pat her right thigh—another sign. I watched her out of the corners of my eyes.

She had once been a beautiful woman who loved life, but years of sadness and disappointment had taken their toll. With the deaths of six of her children, her love of life died. When her "people," as she called the slaves, walked away as soon as the Yankees showed up, she could not believe they left her. She had thought they all loved her. Only Old Moll and two or three older ones stayed.

She never looked happy. Even when she smiled it wasn't really a smile; it was little more than a twitch of her lips and cheeks. When anyone spoke to her, she tended to look down or to the side. As I am remembering her, I think of rain clouds or ashes. And there were times when she frightened me. The beginning of her spells had started long ago when we lived in Charleston.

By five forty-five all the guests had arrived.

Mama was standing in the opened entrance looking down the lane. "Sometimes he's so un..." Her voice trailed off. Beads of sweat were on her forehead. The pitch of her voice was changing. Her eyes were getting larger. Wisps of hair worked loose onto her forehead. She was rapidly patting her thigh. Since the deaths of my sisters I had seen these signs come upon her—only for days sometimes—but then there were times when she wasn't her real self for a month. My father had no patience with her when she was like this. After loud threats he would order Old Moll—who had been Mama's maidservant since she was a little girl—to take her to the little room at the rear of the house; its walls were thick and the door heavy. It had no window.

Mama looked at the hall clock again, leaned forward, peered into the parlor. Everyone was drinking and talking. She turned and looked at me. Her large eyes stared into mine. They did not blink. "Edmund, you need to go over there and get him," she whispered. Her voice had deepened, as it always did when one of her spells was about to come on her.

But just as she spoke, Mary came out of the parlor and, hearing her, said, "No need to; I've already sent Ben."

And it was at that instant we heard his screams, growing louder and louder, as he came running toward the house, "Mama. . .Mama...Granpa's shot hisself...Granpa's shot hisself!"

My father never talked about his parents. Only once did Mama mention them. I don't recall why or when she did. It may have been when I was sitting with her in the little room. I only remember her suddenly saying, "Your father's mother was cruel." That was all.

All I know of his early life is that he was from Scotland and in 1818 shipped from Liverpool to Charleston where he started a sugar store. In a few years he made enough money to become a slave trader, though he always referred to himself as a "broker." Selling Negroes made him wealthy.

In 1825 he built a fine house on the harbor and married Rachael Bondurant, the only daughter of a prominent French Hugenot family in Charleston. She brought him more wealth.

I was born in 1831. Before I was born my father named me Benjamin Edmund Magruder. He was certain I would be a boy. I was to be called "Edmund," the name of his father's father. But when I came, and he saw me as I was, I know he wished I had been stillborn, for he detested all things imperfect and I was more than imperfect. A large red birthmark covers the left side of my forehead, spreading down across my cheek and ear. My left leg is two inches shorter than my right so that I have to wear a built-up shoe and walk with a jerky motion. My speech is slow and hesitant; when I become anxious I stammer so that I appear dull of wit. Nothing about me resembles my father. I am short with small bones and have curly black hair and facial features similar to my mother's. Except for my impairments and her spells, I have always felt that she and I were almost the same person.

Ten months after my birth, mother had another boy but he was dead. Four years later my twin sisters were born and after them in the next five years my brothers, Robert and John, came.

Death lives with our family. In 1841, a yellow fever epidemic killed my pretty little sisters, just as they turned six. Their dying was horrible. I wasn't allowed to go near them so I didn't see it, but Mama told me about it during one of her spells: "My precious little babies were all healthy and happy one day and then they had sweats and headaches and their skin was reddish. Then they turned yellow and vomited, over an' over, and I couldn't stop it and, oh, God, Edmund, streaks of blood ran out of the corners of their eyes and mouths. They suffered continuously for seven days and nights. I didn't leave their sides: cooling them with wet cloths, changing their soiled nightdresses and sheets, reading their favorite stories and praying and begging God to save them. But He didn't...I couldn't understand why He didn't save them. My love for Him should have saved them. And then they died and were buried in the city cemetery.

"Then it came to me—what killed them. I had seen it. The night before my babies first came down with the fever, it came to their room in the dark and stood in the doorway looking into where they lay. It stared at them. It stood there for the longest time with its mouth opening wide, then closing over and over. It was saying something I couldn't hear. It just stood there, staring and moving its lips. I could almost see its face in the candlelight. It was strong looking, tall, straight, and well dressed like a gentleman. For an instant, as it turned from the doorway, its face was clear. I saw that which called itself *Benjamin Lucretius Magruder*. Now, I know it for what it truly is. I know what killed my babies."

I never saw a tear in Father's eyes when my sisters died, nor one when they were buried. You would have thought nothing had happened. His face, his voice, his words were, as always, empty of sadness or concern for Mama, much less for me.

I could not stop crying, yet he never dried my tears, never hugged or kissed me. He never said a word. Tears were streaming down Mama's face and he never took her hand. He did not touch us. He did not like to touch or be touched, not even by Mama. He never struck me and I am certain he never struck her. If a slave needed to be whipped, the whipping was given by one of his overseers. While I know of no one, white or Negro, he ever physically hurt, he was the cruelest man I have ever known.

He and Mama slept in separate rooms. Every morning, exactly at four o'clock, he got out of bed. By five o'clock, he had shaved, washed, combed and neatly parted his reddish-brown hair, and dressed in one of his dark suits and weskits tailored in London. The slightest speck of lint was brushed away. His shoes gleamed. He was fastidious in all things: appearance, speech, behavior, and, most especially, in his business dealings.

He was taller than other men, straight and broad-shouldered, with large hands. His body was strong. But it was his cold, deep-set, dark brown eyes, heavy brows, thin lips and sharp-boned face that intimidated anyone who came near him. When he stood before you with his eyes on yours, you did not oppose him—ever.

Once, long ago, as I looked at him, all I saw was darkness and so I have thought of him ever since as darkness.

In public, he presented himself as he wished to be seen: Not as a vulgar, uneducated dealer in human flesh with tobacco juice dripping from the corners of his mouth; but rather, as a man of substance, refined and well-mannered, a man of honor who tithed to the church and was a gentleman of the first order.

His belief was not in God, but in the one who was cast out. I am certain that if he ever prayed it was to that one. As with many things, he deceived others into believing that he was a man of faith. Soon after we arrived in Maury County in 1842, he became a communicant at St. John's Episcopal Church. Religious practices meant nothing to him. He came to church only on Easter and Christmas and then he usually slept through half the service. Once, after an Easter service, I heard Reverend Carpenter ask him, "Mister Magruder, since my sermon today was on the eternal blessings of God upon man, I am interested in your opinion, sir."

Father's face flushed and turned to stone. His eyes narrowed. He looked at Reverend Carpenter for a long moment, as though not comprehending what the reverend had asked, or as if he was looking at a fool. Then he said, "My opinion, sir...my opinion to your exceedingly prolonged sermon about what you call 'the eternal blessings of God'...my opinion, sir, is that I am starving and must get home to eat."

After the burial of my sisters, Father left immediately for Savannah with a large coffle of slaves for the market.

The next morning, Mama called me into her bedroom. She was looking into the mirror on her dressing table. She pointed to her right eye.

"Edmund, does this eye look higher than the other one?"

"What?"

"Pay attention! Look at my eyes! Does the right one look higher than the left?"

I leaned forward and looked. "No, ma'am, they both look the same."

"Oh! Well...well, you go on and eat something. I'm not hungry."

I did not see her again until that night at the dinner table. She said nothing when she came in and sat down across from me. She laid her Bible beside her napkin. I was so hungry I wasn't paying any attention to her. Then Old Moll brought in a plate of biscuits but didn't set them down. She just stood beside Mama looking down at her. I was reaching for the molasses when I realized something was wrong and looked over at Mama. Her forehead was shimmering with sweat. She was staring into the candle flames. At first, I thought the flickering flames were making her eyes tremble. Then, I saw they were flitting back and forth at each of the candles then down at her Bible so quickly that they seemed separate from her. Her lips were moving as though she were speaking but there was no sound.

"Miss Rachael, what's the matter with you, baby?" asked Old Moll.

Mama didn't respond. Her eyes continued their rapid movements.

"Mama, look at me! What's wrong?" I asked loudly.

This time her eyes fixed on mine. For an instant, she did not seem to recognize me. Then, she shook her head and said, "Oh, Edmund, honey, pass me the greens."

The next day, I was out in the front yard watching ants eat a sparrow I had killed, when she hollered through the open parlor window, "Edmund, come in here for a minute and help me."

As I ran into the room, Old Moll was standing off to the side shaking her head, with her face all knit up as though she was about to cry. Mama was sitting in her rocker, in front of the fireplace, staring into a hand mirror, turning her head, first one way then the other. "Come over here next to me, Edmund...Old Moll keeps telling me I'm wrong, but she can't see worth a hoot anymore. Now, get right up close here and look at my nose."

I leaned against her. She smelled good. She always did. I loved to feel her body touching mine. Some nights, when Father was away, she would let me sleep with her. I would always press myself against her.

She held the mirror closer and touched the right side of her nose. "See how it's bent to the right and looks like it's broken. It makes me look strange...see it right there?"

I squinted and peered at her nose and saw nothing. I stepped back, "Mama, your nose looks just like it always has."

Instantly, her eyes turned angry. She threw the mirror in the fireplace, breaking it to pieces and without a word left the room. That night she did not come down to eat. The next day she seemed herself again. But her face was unhappy.

As the years passed, her "spells" came only once or twice a year. But when they came, they always scared me. During one, she stuffed herself with food. She ate and ate and ate saying, "Oh, I'm so thin." Twice, I saw her stick her fingers down her throat until she vomited. Then, she might fast for days. If I came into her bedroom in the evening, she would turn to me and say, "My precious boy, do you think I'm still a little beauty?"

Before my sisters died Mama was called a "petite belle" by her Charleston friends. She was a little bit of a thing, more girl than woman in size. Her face sparkled. Her high voice and smile made everyone but Father smile. Tiny, coal-black curls lay all around her face. When I was a boy I thought of her as a girl. I loved her. As I grew older I loved her more.

But, Ben, you've seen how she was. Unhappiness never left her face, always staring as though she was somewhere else; seldom speaking to any of us; barely attending to her appearance; wandering the house at night, quoting scriptures and praying out loud. Only when she went to church or a funeral would she fix herself up and put on a front as though all was well.

In April 1861, Robert and John joined the First Tennessee and left home, never to return. I was given an exemption since I oversaw so many Negroes that were raising cotton and food. There was lots of money to be made during the war. If it hadn't been that he needed me to keep the plantations producing, Father probably would have gotten the army to take me, even with my limp, hoping I would be killed.

A year later, almost to the day of my brothers entering the army, word arrived that John had been killed at Shiloh. The Yankees buried him in a mass grave on the battlefield. My God, the grief that came to Mama and Old Moll. Father was away in Memphis where he was half owner of *Magruder and Powell,* the largest slave brokerage company in Tennessee. Once he was there he usually took a coffle of slaves down to replace those who had died or were worn out on his two plantations in Mississippi. He was gone for three months.

The day after we learned of John's death, Mama came into the library where I was updating Father's account book. Suddenly, she walked over to the desk, closed the book and said, "Edmund, the Devil is doing this to try to get me to curse God."

"What's that, Mama?"

"Taking all my babies away."

I got up and hugged her. "No, Mama, don't say that. It wasn't the Devil; John was killed by the Yankees." I gave her a kiss on the cheek and sat back down. "Now, while I finish up, why don't you go lie down and get some rest."

She reached down and opened the account book, bent over it, squinting her eyes at what was written there. Her eyes moved from left to right, as though she were reading. For a moment, I looked away. When I looked back, she was gone.

My brothers were more like Father than Mama. They were handsome, strong and reserved. Early on, Father took them with him to slave sales and to his plantations in Mississippi. They had little to do with me. To them, I was the same as I was to our father, little more than the smartest Negro he owned. I was tutored with them at the house for one year, but come the day of my twelfth birthday, he put me to work in the fields.

When John turned sixteen, he and Robert left for Harvard and I stayed home. If not for Mama's teaching me at night, I would never have learned to read and write or known mathematics well enough to keep the plantation accounts. Though Father instructed her to teach me all I was able to learn, I am certain he did not believe it would be much, for he was convinced I was unable to understand anything complicated.

Except for my ability to drive Negroes in the field and make them work and make money, I was a pariah to him as, increasingly, I was to my brothers who were becoming more and more like him.

Mama was my only refuge. As I grew older, I became more like her, seldom smiling, wondering why God let us be hurt. She began to share her hidden thoughts with me. As I heard them I felt her coming into me. As it grew stronger I began to see and smell and hear and know all that she saw and smelled and heard and knew. One day, as we sat on the bench under the rose arbor, she took my hand and said, "All of this is God's providence to test me as He did Job; He put Satan here, in my house, under my roof."

On planting day in the spring of 1844, Father gave me a whip and made me a driver of fifty Negroes. He had been preparing me for this since he first sent me to the fields. For five years, I had worked beside them from dawn until the horn was blown at dusk; I sweated and was dirty and stank like they did. But the day the whip was put in my hand and I was made a driver, it came as easy for me to whip a Negro as it was to whip a mule.

Then, on a sunny summer day on my eighteenth birthday, I was given a chestnut saddle horse to ride beside the overseer, so I could learn his ways: how he worked the fields, cared for the stock, kept the Negroes fit, and oversaw everything necessary to till and plant the land, then harvest it for money.

In 1855, when I was twenty-eight and married, with a new baby—you, Ben—Father named me overseer of all three thousand acres and two hundred and sixty-seven slaves. His giving me that responsibility caused me to believe that one day part of it would be mine. But I should have known that while I gave orders to all those Negroes, I did not own the shadow of a single one of them. Not one thing of all that my father owned would ever be mine—not a house, not a barn, not a horse, cow, or one boll of cotton, not even one small clod of all the clods of dirt that held my sweat.

I discovered this soon after Robert was killed at Nashville in December 1864. Father was away delivering slaves to a plantation outside Montgomery. I had gone to his office to write in the *Slave Birth Register* the names of three children born during the past week. Lying there, on top of the desk, was his will. It was open, as though he wanted me to read it.

And I did. Only then was I convinced that what Mama had been telling me was true. I picked it up and read:

"*Be it known that all of my lands, including my two plantations, Glenhaven and Glenmor in Maury County Tennessee, and my two plantations, Glenfernate and Glenbarr in Issaquena County Mississippi, and all of my livestock, farm machinery, crops in the fields and those harvested to be sold; and all of my Negroes; and my half of the brokerage company, Magruder & Powell, in Memphis; and all of my stocks, bonds and money shall go in equal portions to my sons, Robert Disharoon Magruder and John Hamilton Magruder; and that they shall dutifully see to the paying of any and all of my outstanding debts; and that they shall care for my wife, their mother, Rachael Bondurant Magruder, until her death; and that my son, Benjamin Edmund Magruder, and his family shall be allowed to live rent-free in the old overseer's house at*

Glenmor and that he shall be paid commensurate to his work so long as he faithfully executes his duties.

Written by my hand and witnessed by the two signatories below my name on this May 17, 1861.

Benjamin Lucretius Magruder
Witnessed by:
Thomas Finch
James Syler

Below this, in his hand writing, is the following addition:

Be it known now that as my sons Robert Disharoon Magruder and John Hamilton Magruder have both died in the war, I now by this addendum to my will make it known that it is my wish that Robert Edward Magruder, son of Robert Disharoon Magruder, and that James Calhoun Magruder, son of John Hamilton Magruder, shall receive all of my land, slaves, houses, livestock, and all other of my possessions in the same equal portions as their fathers would have had they lived; and that they shall see to the care of my wife, Rachael Bondurant Magruder, and son, Benjamin Edmund Magruder, as defined in my will of May 17, 1861.

So written by my hand on January 24, 1865.

Benjamin Lucretius Magruder
Witnessed by:
Thomas Finch
James Syler

As I read, I smelled the sulphur from his mouth. It rose from the paper. I blew my nose and spat on the floor. I had never believed in demons for I did not believe one word of the Bible; it was all superstition, made up by men who made their living creating tales to explain the awfulness of life and how the next life would be better if you gave them money. But Mama taught me I was wrong, for she had seen a demon, had touched it, smelled it, and taken it into herself.

And over time, as I listened to her, there came into me images and sounds like those within her. As I reread the will I realized that all that she had been telling me was true—and that a demon was living among us.

The day after she learned John had been killed at Shiloh, Mama began taking laudanum morning, noon, and night. Mostly, it calmed her. But when Robert was killed in Nashville two years later, it was little better than water. She wandered from room to room, praying loudly, over and over, "Dear God, protect me from the evil one, cast him out into the fire, save me from the roaring lion...slay the serpent." Some days this went on for hours. Afterwards, she slept half a day, sometimes the entire day.

The old Negroes still on the place after Robert's death, were so scared of her they avoided coming to the house; if they had to, they never looked at her face, especially her eyes. Only Old Moll could comfort her. If Father happened to be here, he had her give Mama laudanum until she passed out. He couldn't tolerate her spells. A few weeks before his birthday, he had a doctor come from Columbia to examine her. The doctor said she had *religious monomania* and should be put in the asylum in Nashville, but as it was occupied by the Yankees the only thing that could be done was to increase the laudanum when she became too excited. And if she became uncontrollable, he told Father to lock her up somewhere where she couldn't hurt herself or escape.

Three nights after Robert's death, Father sent a Negro over to tell me to come quick and help him with Mama.

He was standing in the open front door when I tied my horse to the post by the porch. As I limped up the steps he snapped, “Damnit, boy, can’t you move any faster than that?” Without answering, I stepped inside the entrance hall as he continued, “She’s in the parlor and has wrapped her arms around my Grandfather clock and says she’ll pull it over if I try to take her out…Dr. Lester’s right, she’s crazy as she can be and needs to be put away but, until we can, I want her locked up in that back room. Now you get in here and help Old Moll!”

I did. I gently gripped Mama’s arms. She resisted for a moment, then gave way to Old Moll and me patting her and telling her we loved her and that everything would be all right. We took her to the small room off the kitchen. The thick walls and door muffled her loud praying and pleading. When we were finished, Father gave the keys to Old Moll and said, “If she gets out you’ll be sorry.”

Every night after that, when I left the fields, I went to see Mama. Usually, toward nightfall she calmed. We would talk. Then, in that little cramped room on a steamy August night, she suddenly said, “He sleeps with Negroes. He’s done it since the day we were married.” She told it matter-of-factly, as though she were talking about something she had read in a novel. But she was speaking of her husband, my father. For a moment I couldn’t comprehend it but then I knew, as she touched my cheek, that it was true for she never lied to me. I felt such a terrible sadness for her and—after the sadness—there came a great hatred for my father.

A few evenings later, as I entered her room, her eyes were wide and her hand was rapidly patting her thigh. She jumped from her bed and gripped my hands and said, “Edmund, do you know there are demons in him? Do you want to know how they got into him?" The words rushed from her, as she struck her thigh as fast as her hand would go. "They came from all those Negroes he's laid with. You know how they worship demons from where they come from. And...and...you know how he hates to get dirt on himself...well, he'd come in with dirt on his hands and knees from where he'd been laying on one of them out in the fields. I've seen it...I've seen it...I've seen the dirt as black as they were on his knees and hands, and I could smell their stink on him...Lord God, the stink. You know those people aren't human like us, they've got demons inside of them. That's how they got in him. They entered him when he was on top of them. They came up in his thing. No telling how many he's got in him."

As she talked, I could see what she saw; I could see what had been beyond my understanding. As I listened, her words came into me and became part of me; all that had been was revealed–all those years since the ones I could first remember—when my father shunned me, when he had not loved me and would never love me. All those years, I had been able to believe it was only because I was not made right, that all of me was an ugliness he could not bear. And because of what was revealed, I knew that nothing that was his would ever be mine. Nothing. Nothing. Especially his love.

To protect himself, he would have put Mother away from sight forever–for she knew who he really was.

Ben, you probably wonder why I have not said more about your mother. I can only say it is because I know little about her other than she is a good woman and keeps God's commandments. We are so different. The only thing we share is our love for you. I am comforted knowing she will raise you to be a good man.

I had hoped that killing my father would have killed the demons and protected you, but it is not yet dead. This morning when I was shaving, I saw in the mirror that my birthmark is gone and my hair has turned reddish-brown. I spoke to the mirror. My stammer is gone. That which was in my father is growing in me. It will soon become me, as it did with Mama. I have killed that one in her. Now, my dear mother will never be locked away. I am sorry Old Moll tried to stop me. I no longer trust myself. Father's derringer lies on the desk in front of me. It will now destroy the last one.

Goodbye, Ben.

I love you.

Benjamin Edmund Magruder
November 17, 1865

How We Helped Win WWII

Cast of Characters

Billy Bob ....(12) The oldest of our group, our heavily freckled leader ruled over us with his fast fists.

TC....................... (11) When it came to creating disgusting deformities, he was the master with his eyelids turned inside out.

Bush.................... (11) My best buddy, whose devout Catholic family—who drank all kinds of alcohol openly—saved me from many prejudices.

Double M .... (11) Living all the way over on the next street, he was not quite a full member but he had the best climbing trees and a barn.

GE....................... (10) I was the youngest, the chubbiest and the quickest to come up with ideas for devilment.

I don't remember if what I'm about to tell happened at the beginning, middle, or end of that glorious summer of 1946 when I got a whipping almost every week for something I did that was so wonderful I can still hear it, smell it, and feel every speck of it sixty-five years later.

WWII—more than God—cast its shadow around my world and the worlds of my four boyhood friends while barely touching the edge of our day-to-day lives. Not one of our fathers was in the service. Not one of our mothers was a "Rosie The Riveter." The heavy droning of bombers, the thundering of artillery and the screams of wounded and dying were oceans away. Fire and falling walls, the stench of blood and decay, the gaunt faces of hunger, the gaping mouths and crushed bodies were the lives of other boys. Our war—the war we saw—was in *Life* and *Movietone* newsreels, in newspapers and the happy faces of soldiers and sailors on our streets, and in the occasional jeeps and trucks on our streets and the planes and gliders that flew over us; and there were ration stamps, Victory Gardens, and Uncle Sam posters; and there was Mr. Wright who lived two houses down from us, who was our volunteer Air Raid Warden who wore a helmet and sometimes let us walk with him when he checked on "blackout nights" to be sure curtains and shutters were drawn and closed so no lights would guide German or Jap bombers to bomb our homes. The shadow of war was so far away it never nightmared our sleep. It was not real. Our world was summertime and Christmas and laughter and the adventures of our play.

Finally the war ended.

But not for us.

All of my uncles had come home safely from the Army, Navy, and Air Force. Nobody I knew had been killed. Though I've never breathed a breath of this to anyone until now, inside my head I was more than slightly disappointed that not one relative—even if only a second, third, or fourth cousin—had given his life on the field of battle, or in the air, or on the high-seas and then, after several rounds of rifle fire and bugle-notes, had been buried with full military honors at sea or in a national cemetery. It was an early lesson in life; that you don't always get everything you dream about.

Johnny Banner, the only brother of Betty Banner—the prettiest girl on our street or, for that matter, on every street for miles around—had returned home from Europe. He'd been all over France and Germany reporting for the Stars and Stripes. It's still hard to believe; he came home loaded with all kinds of neat Nazi-German war stuff, which he gave to my buddies and me. My buddies being: Bush and TC, who each got a German army raincoat that snapped together to make a two man pup tent, and Billy Bob who got a mess-kit, and Double M who got an ammunition belt. But, I think it was because he knew I was madly in love with his sister—even though she was twelve and two years older than me—that he gave me the absolutely, positively, most perfectly, splendid thing an American boy could get: a German helmet with a bullet hole smack dab in middle of the front and, to add to its splendor, there was what looked like real blood stains inside around the hole.

In my mind, what Johnny Banner did ranked him right up there with Tom Mix, the Green Hornet, and Superman as one of my heroes. And Betty? Well she was the first and only love of my young heart, a heart that—except for mothers and aunts who didn't count—had not yet known a real woman, nor the love that comes from loving a real woman.

Then there was TC's uncle. We all wished he had been ours. Whether he was trying to or not, with his clipped mustache, dimpled chin, and wide grin he looked a lot like Clark Gable except he didn't have Gable's big ears. He was a real "Flying Tiger" Ace in China where he had flown P-40s with a shark's face and big teeth painted on their front. He knocked down fourteen Jap Zeroes from the sky. You'd think that killing Japs the way he did that the furthest thing from his mind would have been a young nephew back in Tennessee. I met him only once and then only for a few minutes. He tousled my hair and I felt like I had received a blessing. He must have been another special kind of man like Johnny Banner for he brought back something for TC that was extra special nice, but nowhere near my German helmet with German blood around the bullet hole.

When he gave TC a Chinese warrior's bow and a quiver full of arrows with sharp iron arrowheads, I thought TC's eyes were going to pop out of his head. Inside of the bow, near the handle, was a Zen saying written in Chinese. Though it didn't look like real writing to me his uncle could read the stuff. First, he read it in Chinese, which sounded a lot like metal clanging together. Then, he read it in American, "*In the case of archery, the hitter and the hit are no longer the opposing objects, but one reality.*" That made absolutely no sense: to me nor to any of the others. No one asked, "What's that mean?" We just squinted our eyes seriously at it and nodded like we knew.

TC was an absolute archery fiend. He was good at it. All five of us had bows but his was a "Bear" a real Fred Bear bow. As soon as he got it he wanted to show it off. It was the real stuff. He took it to the backyard to try it out. I couldn't even bend it. Billy Bob's arms shook so hard he let go and the bow string smacked him on his forearm so hard he let out a "Dad gum it!" and almost swore but caught himself because TC's mother was hanging out clothes. The arrows had long feathers. You could kill a deer with them, or a Jap, or a Nazi. The bows the rest of us had were either homemade or cheap things made for shooting at paper targets. They could make a dog yelp but that was about all.

We were at the Cussin' Tree. We'd just finished the Camels Bush had stolen from his sister's hiding place. It was mid-morning. A breezy day. We stood there wishing we had more Camels. And thinking. Trying to come up with the day's adventure. Then, out of the blue, Double M, who was not known for coming up with masterful plots and brainy plans, said, "Let's paint our kites like Stuka dive bombers an' shoot the Huns from the sky…Lets use our bows an' arrows and BB guns like artillery and machine guns." He called the Germans "Huns" because that's what his grandfather who had fought in WWI called them.

Still no one spoke. Our brains were turning what he said over, slowly at first, then quickly, it began to take shape and there it was—Double M's blazing idea shooting straight up into the sky.

With a slight hint of admiration, Billy Bob said, "Well, I'll be damned Double M! I didn't even think you had a brain. Let's get those Nazis."

The rest of us followed up with *our* 'I'll be damns.'

"Let's kill those Krauts!" chimed TC.

"Shoot their Heinies from the sky!" Bush and I said together and burst out laughing. We loved the word "Heinie."

We knew we had the day by the tail. And to top it off, the wind was picking up.

"Well, I'll be damned!" Billy Bob repeated.

"That's a bully of an idea," Bush said, whose father was always quoting Theodore Roosevelt.

"A real bully of an idea," I echoed. Next to mine, Bush's father was my favorite of my friends' fathers.

"Ok, everybody, go get your bows an' arrows an' BB guns. I'll bring my kite. Who else has got one?" asked Billy Bob.

"I have," said Double M, raising his hand.

"Me too," chimed TC.

"An' me too," I said

"And I'll bring some paint an' brushes from my dad's shop so we can paint 'em. I'll see ya'll back here. Everybody hurry like hell," said Billy Bob, as he bent down and crawled through the secret passageway we had cut in the hedge that surrounded our refuge from our parents.

"Alright men," Billy Bob commanded, "Get your weapons an' hurry back to your battle stations. *Double time it!*"

The summer before, we had sworn to our parents that we would only shoot our bows in our backyards when an adult was present. We made lots of promises to our parents during those years, but the "backyard promise" we halfway meant after TC almost killed me.

It started out as a pleasant afternoon in my backyard. My parents were away. We decided to play *Chicken*. The idea was: we would lie on our backs in the grass and not move and TC would shoot a steel-tipped arrow straight up in the air; as the arrow returned anyone who jumped or rolled away was a "Chicken." And, anyone who didn't move was either: a hero, a wounded hero, or a dead hero. Three times the arrow shot skyward. Three times we were all Chicken. Then, on the fourth, I didn't move. I squeezed my eyes shut and said a quick prayer, *Dear God, my mother loves me and she loves you too. Save me!* There was a thud. *The arrow has struck me in the heart. I have only one more breath, only one more thought left in me, 'Mama! There was a scream far back in my head, but it wouldn't come out. Why would my mouth not scream? I am dead. That's why. I am dead!*

Then came a scream. A real scream.

"*EEEEEEEEEEE!!!*"

But, it wasn't my scream leaving my head. It was Cornelia's, our maid's scream, "*Oh, my dear Lord Jesus! EEEEEEEEEEE!!!*"

I could hear her pounding feet, her heavy breathing coming closer and closer. I still hadn't opened my eyes. I couldn't. I was afraid of what I would see sticking out of me.

The last tremor of the scream and the last deep gasp for air was ten inches above my face. Then, strong hands gripped me by the shoulders and I was lifted from the ground and hugged so tightly against Cornelia's big bosoms I thought I was going to die, not from an arrow, but from bosom suffocation.

The only time Cornelia ever whipped me was on that day as she was dragging me by my hand back to the house; all the while declaring, "You done scared me ta death...You done scared me ta death...You get in that house now an' you ain't goin' out ag'in 'til yo mama an' daddy gets back." Then came the three blows; they were more like the pats you give someone you love who needs comforting.

But that night, when my parents returned, my mother's laying on of hands was not a patting. And, as always, she honored that perverse pact of our mothers and called the others to report our most recent act of savagery. So, once again, before we could have our suppers, each of us had to add another promise to our long list of promises, "I swear to never ever again..."

❧

We were out of breath when we got back with our weapons to the Cussin' Tree. God had heard our prayers. We had gotten away with our bows and BB guns and kites without being seen.

With his bow and quiver over his shoulders, Billy Bob stooped low as he came through the hedge that surrounded the Cussin' Tree. He carried a large, well made, bright-red kite, two cans of paint, and a dried-out paintbrush gripped between his teeth.

We were waiting there for him with three kites, four BB guns, and five bows. TC had wrapped cloth around the heads of two of his arrows. Sticking above his back pocket I could see the spout of a lighter fluid can. The time for all-out war had come. We were going to save our nation and the good people of the world. But first—

"Holy Jerusalem, Billy Bob, where'd you get that?" asked Bush pointing at the red kite. "It's a beaut!"

"Un-huh," said Double M, without his lips moving.

Billy Bob: put the cans and brush on the ground and held the kite up, turning it slowly for us to admire and long for.

"Mama got her for me for my being so good. Today, it'll be flown by Red Baron the Second, son of the legendary Red Baron, Germany's greatest WW I ace."

"Did you say you got it for being good?" asked Double M.

"Man, you pulled one over on your mama," I said.

We all laughed.

Billy Bob's eyes got hard and his fists doubled up. We shut up. "OK, let's get 'em painted and in the air," he hissed.

He opened the cans. One contained a putrid green paint; the other black. Three kites lay beside the buckets.

Most Nazi planes were painted that exact same putrid green; with black crosses on their wings. Billy Bob went to work. In no time the kites were painted. They were ready to lift from the earth and rain death and destruction on civilization and the people we were sworn to defend.

With weapons and Stukas in hand we went to the field beyond the hedge. It was covered with weeds and scrub-brush, once part of a long-gone, green golf course. It was sided by three streets that, except for mornings and afternoons, had little traffic. Only a few houses looked down through a screen of trees onto the field. The battle we were about to unleash would not be interrupted by the real enemy–grown ups.

"Bush, you and GE fly the planes and the rest of us 'ul do the shootin'"

"Damn, Billy Bob, I wanta shoot too," I said.

"Well, somebody's gotta fly the planes...tell you what, ya'll do the flyin' an' I've got two extra cigarettes I'll give you."

"Now?"

"No, not now, dummy, after the battle."

"Well, how 'bout a half one now?"

"Damnit, GE, you'll get it when it's over. Now, get the planes up in the air."

Their motors roaring, the Stukas hurtled down the airfield and soared into the air. The blitz-krieg had begun. Explosion after explosion came nearer and nearer. Smoke rose in the distance. We could hear them approaching. Billy Bob shouted, "*Are you ready men?*" And then–there they were against the blue sky, the black crosses like the markings of death. They rolled from the sky, one after another, shrieking downward, their machine guns flashing fire like sparklers. "*Give 'em hell!*"

Pffit-Pffit-Pffit, the bullets whipped past our ears, striking all around us, kicking up dust, cutting through small saplings, ricocheting off rocks; the noise of the diving planes and machine guns was deafening. "*FIRE-FIRE-FIRE!*" They opened up with their rifles. They had no effect. The roar of the planes was deafening. Everyone was yelling.

The dive-bombers rose from their first strafing run then, they turned and came straight back.

Bush pointed at the lead Stuka, "*Get 'im! Get 'im!*" Side-by-side, they fired as fast as they could cock them and pull the triggers. It zoomed right over their heads. We could see the bullets striking but nothing happened. It rose with the others and began to make another turn.

"*Load the artillery...we got to get those Krauts!*"

They laid the BB guns down, picked up the bows and quickly strung arrows.

"*Here they come again,*" Double M hollered.

The first one zipped over untouched. The second one got by. But, as the third Stuka started to stoop, TC fired and, suddenly, the bomber came to a halt in mid-air; the arrow struck its cross-frame breaking it in two. It shuddered to a stop and then, shaking back-and-forth, fell to the earth.

"Well, I'll be damned!" said Billy Bob.

And the rest of us followed up with our, I'll be damns.

They reloaded. And waited.

TC brought the second one down with an artillery shell through the tail.

We began to chant, "*TC, TC, TC!*"

But the last Stuka was piloted by Nazi ace Red Baron the Second. It came roaring down, dodging and twisting, its machine guns firing and firing, spewing death and destruction. As it zoomed over Red Baron the Second leaned out of the cockpit and shot a finger at his enemies.

"*Shoot the son-of-a-bitch, shoot the son-of-a-bitch, TC!*" shouted Billy Bob as he shot a finger back at the bright red dive-bomber as it made its turn; the roar of the engines became a high-pitched scream as it bore down with guns spitting fire.

At that moment, out of the corner of my eye, I saw a red flash. I turned. Six feet away stood TC. He looked like Robin Hood. His left arm straight out, his hand gripping the bow's handle, his right arm crooked back, his fingers pulling the taunt bowstring all the way to its maximum, the arrow's feathers touching his fingers, the front of the arrow's shaft resting on the top of his left hand, the cloth covered arrow-head extended a few inches beyond the front of the bow–*the cloth was engulfed in flame*. TC's face was set in stone, as grim as death; his unblinking eyes fixed on the shrieking Stuka. He held...and held...and held...until I thought he had been hit and was standing there dead.

And then...and then...his fingers twitched and released the string, the arrow shot forward, the flames on its head swept backward as bits of burning-cloth flickered in the air. Like a fiery rocket, the thin arrow's trajectory streaked upward in a diagonal line that struck the plane, breaking it into pieces of fire–but that was not the end–the arrow streaked onward, higher and higher, until it came to the end of its arch where its flame curved downward and downward, falling into dry brush and sedge. Oh, how glorious it was—it burst into a conflagration of fire; the leaping flames and smoke rising higher and higher, with the wind spreading it quickly across the field toward the tree line and the street beyond.

No one spoke or moved.

Then, Bush spoke, “Well, I’ll be damn!”

“Well, I’ll be a double-dog damn!” said Billy Bob.

“Damn...damn...damn...damn!” I couldn’t stop saying, “Damn.”

TC’s eyes stretched wide like he was seeing the end of the world.

And, maybe he was, for in the very next moment people came running out of their houses. Women were standing with their hands over their mouths. Men were running toward the fire with rakes and shovels. There was shouting and a few screams and many curses.

I’d heard preachers preach the world would end in fire; that everything was going to be burnt to a crisp. Maybe this was it. Maybe we were seeing it start. Maybe we had started it. Nobody seemed to notice us. For the moment we pyromaniacs were invisible. People and dogs were running back and forth, a cat was stepped on, there was yowling and howling and, over and over, a crusty old voice tried its best to shout, “Call the fire department...Call the fire department...Call the police...Call everybody!”

Suddenly, between the all the pandemonium and clamor there was a split-second of silence and, in that split-second, there was a high-pitched whimper, “I’ve got to hide.” I looked to my side. TC was pirouetting in a tight circle, his face was the face of terror, “Oh my Lord, Oh my Lord they’re gonna hang me for sure!”

Above his whimpering; above the yelling, and barking, and screeching; above the flames and billowing smoke; above the weeping and gnashing of teeth; from far away, there came the strident sirens of fire engines and police cars racing nearer and nearer.

And then they arrived.

It is the anticipation of death that most often is more feared than when death actually comes. So it was with us. The horrors of torture to extract our confessions, the horrors of coming punishments, the horrors of eternal damnation in hell; these horrors pressed our eyes open in the darkness of our nights. Yes, we would one day be found out and if, on that day, we were not killed outright we would likely be put to the rack. But, it needs to be said that—

No matter our pain.

No matter our tears.

No matter our penance.

We were the heroes who shot down Red Baron the Second.

We were the heroes who helped win WW II.

We were the heroes who helped save the earth.

To this day it is glorious.

Ride to Glory

Billy Bob was literally eaten up with freckles. In certain kinds of light, his skin looked like he had some gosh-awful tropical disease. A thousand more, give or take a couple of hundred, and they would all have run together, turning him into one five-foot tall, skinny freckle. Then we'd likely ended up calling him "Nig," because he'd been permanently browned all over. Of course, calling him "Nig" would have made him fiercer than he was prone to be. For my sake, since Billy Bob was older and tougher than me, it probably saved my life by his not being a total freckle.

TC, Bush, and Double M made up the rest of our gang. Since Double M lived all the way over on the next street, he wasn't quite a full member. Our acceptance of him was helped considerably by his yard having the best climbing trees and an old barn that made a first class clubhouse and a fort when we had BB battles with the Cullum gang who all lived on the other side of Lealand Lane.

Double M and Bush were Catholics, which meant they ate a lot of fish. I've always felt that Fridays must have been hell on them. Maybe I shouldn't admit it, but I got a perverse type of pleasure when I ate cheeseburgers in front of them on Fridays, which I tried to do with regularity. Admit it, we all like having some solid, here-and-now proof that we bet on the right horse when it comes to religion. Any kid will tell you that eating fish every Friday for the rest of your life is not even close to being in the money when it comes to cheeseburgers. It's a wonder they hung with it. If it had been me, I'd have joined another church, just to get the cheeseburgers.

Back then, in the summertime, kids turned out ideas faster than those Old Testament types begat children. When you haven't got television or air-conditioning, and your mama is committed to teaching you the American Work Ethic, it tends to influence creativeness in such ways as getting out of your house without being seen. Those of us that made it, gathered at the "Cussin' Tree."

The Cussin' Tree was a big, old mock orange tree that grew green, bumpy, soft-ball size mock oranges which dripped white sticky stuff when you stuck holes in them. They were hard and heavy and hurt like hell when you used them as hand-grenades. The tree was hidden in a place like Robin Hood might have had in Sherwood Forest. It's where we went to smoke and talk ugly. And it's where Billy Bob came up with the idea of turning our Red Rider wagons into soapbox racers and riding them through a wall of fire. Democratic-type government wasn't Billy Bob's ambition when he was hot on some new and overpowering idea. At those times, his prepubescent squeak ruled over us like a Henry the Eighth bellow, even when we were questioning his judgment on things like walls of fire.

By the time we'd finished the cigarettes that Bush had confiscated from his daddy and pumped ourselves up with some fresh dirty talk, we had Billy Bob's idea roughed out into a plan. I'm telling you, in those days kids were whizzes when it came to creating. If we'd set our minds on better mousetraps, all of us would be rich men today.

Come the next day, we'd replaced the beds of our Red Riders with racing bodies made from wooden crates. Tied to the front wheel axels were guide ropes that turned them quicker than power steering. Needless to say, Billy Bob's had extra "horse-power," that is, an extension on the back for one of us to kneel on while we pushed.

His idea had come from a Movietone film that showed a stunt man smashing his car through a burning barn, then leaping out with his hands clasped high above his head while the crowd roared. As he acted out the leaping, hand-clasping part, I saw a semi-wild, excited look grow on Billy Bob's face, which caused me to tense up. I'd seen it before and had a flash back to the previous winter when I fell through the ice into Mrs. Foy's goldfish pond. On that day, he had turned us all into north-woods trappers. And now, here he was with that same fast-eyed look, telling us all about the glories of riding through a wall of fire.

Double M's street was perfect for setting walls on fire. It had a steep hill, no traffic, and best of all you couldn't see the bottom of the hill from anybody's house. It took awhile for us to drag a pile of cardboard boxes all the way from the back of Landon's Hardware Store to Double M's street. Billy Bob supervised the wall building. After a lot of adjusting to meet his specifications, it was impressive looking. It was four feet deep, eight feet high, and twelve feet wide. From a distance it looked like it would stop a tank.

By now, Billy Bob's movements were starting to get quick all over, like you get when you've just got to take a leak and your surroundings won't allow it. To tell the truth, I was picking up speed too. My muscles were getting jerky and my vision sharper. Now, I was seeing the beauty of it all. That great wall of roaring red, yellow, and white flames rising to heaven, and me and Billy Bob riding through it to safety on the other side, where the cheers of the crowds were waiting for us to leap out with our hands clasped high in the air—as HEROES!

No one was going to push Billy Bob's racer but me. For today we were bound for glory.

We waited at the top of the hill: he, forward, in the driver's seat, legs squeezed down inside the wooden body, knuckles white with gripping the guide ropes; and me, kneeling on the back, one foot on the ground, one leg bent like a taunt bow-string, waiting to shoot toward our target. We waited, our eyes fixed on Bush, "Lighter of the Flame." He lit his newspaper torch and carefully laid the fire around the base of the wall. His movements, the first wisps of flame and smoke, all seemed unreal—slow—silent—sinister, like some ancient preparation for sacrifice. All sound was suspended as I listened for the command. I waited, and then it came—"GO!"

Muscles, bones, nerves, blood, flesh, all that was me released in one mighty heave, with such force that—for an instant—the racer's front wheels lifted from the ground, and then we rocketed down the hill. Traveling at a velocity heretofore unknown by a Red Rider, our racer sped down-down-down, with wheels and wind whirling, as though we must lift from the earth into flight. We were a flash of light, rushing toward Billy Bob's fiery vision, which zoomed upward to strike us. Suddenly, for a final split-second, before my face, there was the roaring, burning, smothering wall of flame. My last thought was a flash image of a black, burned to a crisp, chicken-liver—Me! And then we hit, and were inside, all the fire God had ever made!

AIR—AIR—cool, cool AIR, free of fire, clean of smoke, quiet, sweet tasting—I was out, on the other side, safe and uncharred! I could hear a great, massed cheering from the wonder-struck crowds, and through it all, someone screaming my name. It was Billy Bob. He was on fire! From the top of the wall a single, small box had fallen, flaming, into his lap. He was trapped in the racer and screaming something awful, "*Get it off—get it off—get it off—get it off!*" With his attention seriously diverted, the racer zig-zagged down the street, went into a spin, jumped a ditch and overturned. Dust, wisps of smoke, black flakes, and terrible language rose and spread around the wreckage. I was thrown clear.

TC, Bush, and Double M rushed to the racer and dragged Billy Bob out and began rolling him in the dirt. I crawled toward them and slowly climbed up my legs onto my feet. We helped him stand and began to do our best to separate the dirt and gravel and black bits of charred cardboard from his flesh. He seemed to be totally unappreciative of our efforts, for between groans and whimpers, he'd flail one of us, then another, with the worst cussin' I'd ever heard. But we stuck steady to our task, we all knew there would be hell to pay if Billy Bob went home and his mama looked at him and he didn't look right. For all of our mamas were sworn to some unwritten, but binding, maternal pact of perversity to telephone each other whenever they knew, or even suspicioned that we had been up to no good. For they knew us, they knew that we had a righteous obligation to share with one another, the joys of our sins.

All and all, Billy Bob began looking better, especially after we had spit on our hands and cleaned his face. Double M kept brushing hard, with some leaves, on a big black spot on his t-shirt, until he was rudely pushed away. We stood back to observe our handiwork.

Everyone had hope on his face, especially Billy Bob. Like an artist seeking the slightest flaw on a finished portrait, we looked him up and down.

Nobody moved or spoke. The very silence suggested something dreadful. I looked at TC, Double M, and Bush. Their eyes were stretched big-wide, and the skin on their faces had gone white, loose, and scary. I got sudden, queasy, sick feeling, like a knife was twisting in the pit of my stomach. I looked again at Billy Bob, and there before me was the awful truth of our fiery ride.

Billy Bob's eyebrows were burned plumb off his face.

PONY

The glob of spit shot—out—out—out—and still out until, finally, it curved downward and hit with a—*SPLAT*—two feet beyond a battlefield strewn with spittle. Like a warrior-king, Billy Bob leaned triumphantly back on his elbows. His was the regal smile of one who has again assured his superiority by right of arms.

It was summertime. The five of us and an assortment of dogs were taking up most of the sidewalk in front of Hutcherson's Pharmacy and Landon's Hardware Store. Our stage. Here, like strolling contortionists, we regularly performed our bad habits. There was always a passing audience of grownups to be impressed with our ability to spit, or to witness the extraordinary dexterity required when you tightly pressed a thumb against one nostril—and loudly blew your nose.

When we ran out of spit and mucus, we would saunter into Landon's. Landon's! Military arsenal and weapons' supplier to the summer soldier: B-B guns, pocket knives, cap pistols, bows and arrows, sling shots, pea shooters, and all the materials you needed to make that piece de resistance of summer warfare—rubber guns. Rubber guns fired loops cut from automobile inner tubes. The loops were knotted and stretched tight from the end of the wooden barrel to the clothespin trigger held to the back handle with a band of rubber. Few things in life are more satisfying than hearing the solid whack of knotted rubber hitting the bareback of an enemy playmate. A scream of pain makes it sublime. For the rest of the day, the success of your crafty ambush was there for all to see—a fiery, red whelp. Had we set our ambitions toward cold-blooded mayhem we would have ranked right up there with Attila and Bonnie and Clyde. As it was, our dogs and cats and younger brothers and sisters constantly watched us out of the corners of their eyes, creating in their minds ugly sounds and pictures—the rat-a-tat-tat of machine guns riddling criminals full of holes—like Swiss cheese.

Since the dogs and shoppers were bedazzled by our spitting, they deserved an encore. "Let's do our deformities," said TC and immediately began turning his eyelids inside out. Once turned, they could stay that way for hours. Then, a silly, pompous grin would spread all across his face. He knew he had the rest of us hands down when it came to looking deformed. The rest of us weren't even in the same league. Bush could only bend his fingers back to the wrist and my best was your basic lower-leg-out-of-the-joint walk. But TC was really horrible. You could see it in the startled faces of old ladies who walked hurriedly around us to get in the stores. When you looked at TC dead on, and saw those blood-red strips of raw flesh above the whites of his eyes, it was just about the most sickening thing you can imagine. Today, he wasn't grinning. He had an intense, fixed stare that seemed totally unaware of the rest of us. When I saw both of his eyelids suddenly flip down, I realized he was experiencing something powerful. I followed his gaze. And then, I saw her...

Standing like a golden statue in the summer sun, was a pony standing alone on the school playground across the street. She was stunning—a glowing, palomino pony with a flaxen mane and tail—she was the most beautiful thing I had ever seen. A real, live pony; symbol, nay, the very embodiment of our play: Robin Hood, Mountain Men, Lee, Stonewall Jackson, Tom Mix, Cowboys and Indians, warfare of every sort—and through it all we rode straight and strong, striking our enemies down, right and left and on—to victory! High upon that pony's back we would be able to look down on all the rest of humanity—for they would be beneath us.

Glitters of light surrounded the pony. Double M, who liked to read stories about old-timey days, said the glitter looked just like the halo he had seen in a picture of King Arthur's charger. "Gnats, just a bunch of gnats," Billy Bob pronounced. Billy Bob ruled over our gang with the divine right of quick muscles and preferred to dictate the day's visions. "She looks more like something Forrest would have ridden when he whupped up on them damn Yankees." We played Civil War a lot and, of course he always commanded the winning side—the Rebs. He was either: Lee, Jackson, or Forrest, and sometimes all three in one battle. He said any dummy could see he had to be the commanding general, since he was the only one who had a Confederate general's hat. It was a cheap, felt thing with a Rhode Island Red chicken feather stuck in the band. He liked to call the feather a plume. While I'll have to admit that the hat had style, the truth is that not one of those generals went around with a plume sticking out of his hat. And if he had, it wouldn't have been an old beat-up Rhode Island Red chicken feather.

The pony had not moved. She was totally alone. She was lost! She was ours for the catching, and ours for the riding. And as we were learning the ways of the world, our minds were already calculating that she represented hard, cold cash on the hoof. Such gentle beauty had to be some sweet child's dearest possession. We were assured that, loving his child as he did, some rich daddy would offer a reward, would give us money, for our good deed. Since she had no halter, Billy Bob told us to go into Landon's and buy some rope. He would keep his eye on the pony. In a flash, we were in and out with the rope. And still the pony was there, as real and as beautiful as ever.

Frantically, we set to work on a lasso. The rope was twenty-feet of cotton nightmare. Knot tying is an art, and the only one we had down pat was the standard, impossible to untie except with a sharp knife blade, shoelace knot. All ten hands started twisting, looping, and knotting at the same time. It looked like we were trying to come up with the getting burned by rude rope yanks. That gave way to bad name-calling, then to shoving. We were right on the verge of a free for all when we stumbled onto it. It looked like something that was half-lasso and half hangman's-noose. I know this: if I'd been either a horse or a horse thief, I wouldn't have wanted that thing around my neck. But it was going to have to do, or we were going to end up killing each other.

Then, Billy Bob spoke, his words were chilling, "Double M, since you know so much about horses and chargers and stuff, how about you putting that rope around her neck—we'll back you up."

Well now, when it finally gets down to the actual fitting of your imaginings with your realities, they don't always square at the edges. Movies about cowboys and playing cowboys are one thing, but walking right up to a wild stallion and trying to put a rope around its neck, that's another. A sickly look was concentrating itself on Double-

M's face. I could see his fingers trying to squeeze up and hide in his hands. He began to sag all over, as pure fear turned all his bones and muscles to mush. Billy Bob said, "Double M, you ain't goin' chicken on us now are you?" There it was. Chicken! Better to have bubonic plague, leprosy, or only one leg than to be called, "Chicken." It was a condemnation worse than death, for it marked you for the rest of your natural-born life. Once you were labeled "Chicken" your only options were suicide or moving to another town.

Double M took the rope and, like a man going to his own hanging, struck a death-march pace, as we crossed the street. As slow as he was moving, the rest of us were slower. He was our friend, and we wanted him to have plenty of room to run if he needed it. It was like we were in a slow motion film, a classic scene: the King of the Wild Horses is finally cornered; the relentless sun beats down; the five dust-covered cowboys close in; the brave roper moves cautiously up to the horse's head. If the stallion goes for anyone, it will be him; the time of truth has come! The film slows, then stops on a drama-filled scene of the Old West: At the end of a sun-bleached ravine, five sweat-stained cowboys stand, lean and hard, before a great, wild stallion; one figure holds a lasso right at the point of passing it over and around the stallion's wide-flared nostrils and chiseled head. And then it happened...

The pony flicked her tail, stomped at a horsefly, curled her lips back from her teeth and gave a long-drawn, high-pitched whinny. Double M screamed, dropped the rope and ran smack dab into Bush. As we ran, everyone was hollering. I could hear a strange whimpering coming from my throat, and Billy Bob kept saying, "Dear God, save me…dear God save me."

When we were safely back inside Landon's, and in the back of the store, we turned to see if the frenzied beast was coming straight on through the glass window to kill us all. Double M was so scared he was stuttering, "D-D-Did you see th-those teeth? They c-could have r-r-ripped my arm off my b-b-body!"

Sucking hard for air, Bush gasped, "Those hoofs could have kicked our brains out."

Since the plate glass was holding firm. Billy Bob said, "TC, Go up there and see what that thing is doing."

TC said firmly, "Ununh, I ain't going by myself. You gotta come with me!"

There was a pause, and then Billy Bob said, "O K everybody, let's go!"

With muscles tensed tight in anticipation of an instant need to leap to safety we eased up to the window and looked out. The pony had not moved. She stood there splendid in the sun. For a moment, no one spoke. Then, Double M, his voice back to normal, whispered, "Hell, she's just a pony. I'm goin' to get her." With shoulders squared, he went right out the door without looking back. By the time the rest of us were across the street, he had the rope around her neck and she was nuzzling his hand.

For the remainder of the day, we led one another around the schoolyard, with one and sometimes two of us sitting upon her broad back. Now and then, we would stop to let her rest and graze. As she munched the green grass we lay around her, admiring her gentleness and all of her loveliness. Her golden coat was soft as silk and when, for a moment, she raised her head to gaze far away, the peacefulness in her eyes gave us joy. It was a day filled with sun—and it was heaven!

But a new problem arose as the sun began to set. Now that we had her, where were we going to put her? TC said, "How "bout Brother Black's?" Brother Black was a Church of Christ preacher who taught at Lipscomb where Billy Bob, TC and I were students. He had a field nearby where he kept horses. It was a double-barreled idea. Being that Brother Black, God, Billy Bob, TC, and I were so closely tied together it would give Brother Black a chance to do a good deed for everyone. And, as Bush and Double M were Catholics, it would be further proof that the rest of us were on the winning side. Not that we really needed it, since their having to eat fish every Friday, for eternity, was plenty of evidence that God didn't look kindly upon them.

When we got to Brother Black's I volunteered to handle the negotiations. Since the Lord is on the side of the righteous, I wanted the lead position in showing Bush and Double M the error of their ways. The congregation waited behind me in the yard as I offered Brother Black the opportunity to strike a blow for the Lord. And then, with a big smile on his face, that Man of God looked down upon us, and in his best preacher-voice, said, "A dollar a day boys, a dollar a day, that's what I charge everybody, and to be fair that's what I'll have to charge you, a dollar a day."

What did he say? Did he say a dollar? A dollar a day? He's supposed to say, "God love you, you fine young fellows, bring that beautiful creature of the Lord's right on in here. Bless *you for giving me this chance to do good. I won't charge you a cent. For it is written, 'It is more blessed to give than to receive.' Praise the Lord!" What in hell did he just say? A dollar a day? Hell, we ain't got a dollar a week among us. Hellsfireanddamnation! What he just said was, "No!"*

Looking down at my feet, muttering as I stumbled away, "Thanks...we'll see...maybe, thanks a lot." *Hellsfireand-damnation, hellsfireanddamnation.* As I passed Bush and Double M, I hissed, "If either one of you laugh, or say anything, I'll bust you in the nose."

Pony in tow, we returned to the schoolyard, to think.

As we set there in the evening shadows, I was sure I heard a snicker and saw some quick smirks pass between Bush and Double M. *Damn the fairness of greedy preachers–now what are we going to do.*

Finally, Billy Bob spoke up, "Well, we gotta do something and do it quick. The only other place is Mr. Naked's."

We called him "Mr. Naked" because he was an artist who specialized in painting naked women. And if that wasn't bad enough, he had two, gosh-awful, gigantic dogs that could kill and eat a grizzly. He lived in an old, run-down house surrounded by vines and hedges. Just thinking about it started my left eye to twitching. My future prospects suddenly took on a bleakness. If I saw one of those naked women, I'd probably go blind. And if those beasts saw me, I was going to disappear forever down their throats. But we had to risk it. Mr. Naked was our last chance.

I'd just about had all the excitement I could stand for one day. This time, I wasn't volunteering for anything. The fact is, nobody was. When we pushed our way through those dog-fanged hedges, it was going to be all for one and one for all. *Come on pony.*

We stood before the great, walled hedge that surrounded Mr. Naked's house. It was a Dracula film: the wild, forsaken forest of Transylvania., filled with vampires, werewolves, and packs of man-devouring dogs. The night was dark as a wolf's mouth. Bush whispered through his clenched teeth, "You remember those women vampires who slept in those boxes at Dracula's castle...you don't suppose Mr. Naked and those women..."

"Shut up, Bush!" tongue chopped Billy Bob.

I could tell my hearing was sharpening as we crept through the hedges. Listening for the flap—flap—flap of descending wings. *Can vampires hear you heart booming? Damnit, who keeps stepping on the limbs?* They cracked like dry bones. It was the pony. *I may have to kill her. Better her than me.*

Between the rustle and crackle of our footsteps, came a strange, almost imperceptible voice, "Dear Mary Mother of God forgive me, for I have sinned..."

Then another voice, this one near hysteria, "O' Jesus, I think I smell blood!"

"Damnit Bush, shut up!" Billy Bob's voice struggled against a scream.

We were out, and into the yard. In front of us reared a large, ivy-covered, stone house—the castle of Count Dracula. No one moved, our eyes froze on the iron-hinged front door.

The pony whinnied loudly and pawed the ground.

There before us was the maw of the beast. Light flickered through the door's small windows onto a dragon-headed knocker. The dragon's eyes moved with the light.

I heard my voice praying aloud, in unison with Bush and Double M, "Dear Mary Mother of God forgive me for I have sinned...Dear Mary Mother of God...

All I could think of was my throat. When that door opened, how was I going to keep whatever that thing was inside away from my throat? I searched my pockets for a weapon. Nothing. For the want of a cross, or some garlic, or a mirror, or a good sharp stake, I was about to be sucked dry.

Listen! "Click"...a lock turning. *O' my Lord, O' my Lord.* The door handle turned. With the rusty, strident, creaking of a coffin lid, the door slowly—ever so slowly—opened.

Standing in the doorway, outlined by the flickering light, was a tall, silent man; his face shadowed.

O' Lord, O' Lord. Children shouldn't have to die this way. Way down, deep inside of me, I felt the last scream of my life beginning to form. *O'Lord, here he...he...he comes.*

"Hello, boys. Can I help you?"

Count Dracula slyly requesting to fang our throats.

We stood there silent, like five stone statues.

"What's wrong? Has a cat got your tongues?"

Dracula the jokester.

He stepped toward us. But—it was just a normal step forward. Not a soaring leap that went straight to my throat. And his voice—it was normal. Not one of those hisses that turn into the last roaring howl you ever hear. It was just a plain, ole' everyday voice.

With wide-stretched eyes, we examined him. No wings. No cape. No death-white skin. No burning eyes. NO FANGS! Before our eyes, Count Dracula dissolved... disappeared.

And became...Mr. Naked.

"Whatcha got thah, a pony?" he asked.

"Yes sir, Mr. Nak...yes sir, she sure is!" said Bush.

You could see Mr Naked's eyes smiling as he admired her. "She's a beauty. Well boys, I'm guessin y'all might be needin sum help...Y'all are all noddin, 'Yes.' So I'm goin to guess y'all might need a place for that pony to stay. Right?"

The stars were out as we started home. Once, we stopped to hear the pony whinning to us through the darkness. Mr. Naked had put her in his field. Then he had taken us into his barn where he fixed an old bridle and saddle for us to use when we rode her. She could stay there until we found her owner. And got our reward. When we asked what he would charge, he just laughed and said, "Boys, I probably ought to be payin y'all for lettin me keep such a splendid creature." He didn't want a thing. Not a thing. It was free!

As we walked on through that summer night, my mind kept going over and over everything that had happened to us that day. Somehow I knew something important had occurred, something that I could not yet put into words. But later on, way later on, it came to me–*things ain't always the way they appear to be.*

Apaches

(TELEGRAM)

MESCALERO AGENCY, TO COMMISSIONER INDIAN AFFAIRS, WASHINGTON, D. C. AUG. 21ST 1879, WARM SPRING. INDIANS HAVE ALL LEFT THIS RESERVATION GOING WEST. WILL PROBABLY TRY TO INTERCEPT THOSE SUPPOSED TO BE ON THE WAY FROM SAN CARLOS. HAVE INFORMED THE MILITARY.

RUSSELL, AGENT

"These hills are full of Apaches. They've burned every ranch in sight. He had a brush with them last night. Says they're stirred up by Geronimo."

The first words in the movie *Stagecoach*—1939

"They are the keenest and shrewdest animals in the world, with the added intelligence of being human beings."

Major Wirt Davis—1885

When they scalped an enemy they sang one song over it, a special song. The song goes on, "I will get a piece of the enemy's ribs, and I will get a piece of the enemy's backbone for me."

Western Apache Raiding and Warfare—1971

"I was born on the prairie where the wind blew free and there was nothing to break the light of the sun. I was born where there were no enclosures."

Geronimo

"I have killed ten white men for every Indian slain."

Cochise

"This could be good land without the Apaches."

From the movie *Chatto's Land*—1972

On the hottest day of summer, when the sun was directly overhead and scorching the earth, heat waves created images of distant lakes. Everyone was asleep, even the soldiers; no one saw us or heard us; we broke away from our reservations and moved across the earth like the wind.

Of course, our mothers—the reservation agents—knew we were gone, for we had to have their permission to go out and play. Once outside, we became our true selves: marauding, pillaging, burning, wholly irreclaimable, savage killers. Filled with the power of the grizzly and the cunning of coyotes we were five bloodthirsty Apaches on the warpath.

We ran as fast as our legs would carry us to our camp beneath a large mock-orange tree. A thick wild-shrub hedge encircled the camp. It shielded us from any "White Eyes" that might be in pursuit. Normally, we called the tree the "Cussin' Tree" but on this day, Billy Bob said it was to be the "Sacred Tree." He was twelve and the oldest. He could probably have beat up any two of us together at one time. As always, he assumed leadership without any discussion or hint of dissent.

There was one problem about Billy Bob. And it was a big one. He had no eyebrows. They still hadn't grown back since they were burned off the month before. On that day he had convinced us to ride our Red-Rider wagons through a cardboard wall of fire. Having no eyebrows took away some of his ferocity. But only "some" because even though it made his face look a little like an owl I knew he could still kill me with his bare hands.

We sat cross-legged in a circle. Billy Bob stood above us. He began by giving us our names—

"Of course, I'm the only one who can be *Geronimo.*

"TC, you'll be *Cochise.*

"Double M, you're *Chatto.*

"Bush, you're *Victorio.*

"An' Spain, you'll be *Loco.*"

"I don't want that name," I said.

"Well, since you're the craziest one of us…it fits," smirked Billy Bob.

Double M, who didn't even live on our street sniggered and I kicked him and we both drew back and likely would have gotten into it if Billy Bob hadn't ordered, "Damnit, you two, cut it out!"

"Well, I still don't like it," I said.

With that, Billy Bob, who was a good head taller than me, stepped over, leaned down and stuck his freckled face into mine, and in a voice that had a fist in it, said, "*Did you hear what I said? You're Loco an' I'm Geronimo, an' I'm tellin' you to quit whinin'! Loco killed a grizzly with a knife an' was a chief too, just not nearly as famous as Geronimo. You're Loco, got it?*"

"Un-huh."

"One more thing, every time ya'll talk to someone, use their Apache name. OK, that's settled…now get your stuff out."

One by one, we reached into our pockets and paper bags and pulled out what we had pillaged from our homes. We set our loot on the ground in front of us.

"Cochise, did you get the paint?"

"Yea, my sister's toothpaste."

"Chatto, what about the tobacco?"

"Yea, five of my granma's Lucky Strikes."

"Victorio, since your folks are the only ones that drink a lot, did you get the firewater?"

"I got it, but sure as hell my Daddy's gonna know 'cause I had to put an awful lot of water back in the bottles so he wouldn't see how much was gone."

"OK, Loco, what about you?"

I reached into the brown paper bag and pulled out a big handful of white feathers.

There was silence.

"Damn, was white all you could get?" rasped Billy Bob.

"Well, White Leghorns are all we've got in the pen an' I almost couldn't get them 'cause the rooster like to of spurred me to death pullin' his tail feathers out."

"Well, dad blast it, if you couldn't have got some Rhode Island Reds it seems the least you could have come up with was some Dominickers...Ah, hell! Pass out the Leghorns... Give me that big one." He stuck it between the bandana and the back of his head. The rest of us did the same.

"OK, ya'll, look at these pictures I tore out of National Geographic at the library an' do your faces with a white streak across your noses an' cheekbones."

Billy Bob was a nut about Apaches and when it came to Geronimo he was a certified nut. He'd read everything he could get his hands on in libraries, the National Geographic, and comic books. He had seen every movie that had an Apache in it. And he had a photographic memory of everything he had read or seen about them.

"Listen, ya'll! Geronimo was a Chiricahua Apache, so that's what we are. We're Chiricahuas. We're the fiercest of all Injuns."

I leaned over to Bush who was sitting beside me, "Did you hear that dirty word he just said we are?" I whispered the word in his ear.

Bush began giggling loudly and couldn't stop.

"So what's so funny Victorio?" hissed Billy Bob.

"Well, Spain, uh...I mean, Loco, uh, said you just said a dirty word."

"What'n hell, are you talkin' about?

"He said, you said, we are *Cheer-we-ca-cas.*"

With that TC fell over sideways on the ground and Double M started slapping his thighs and we all burst out laughing like hyenas—except for Billy Bob, whose neck was blood red with anger. He was so angry he was about to start bleeding from his nose. And he was silent. And when he got silent we got nervous. His jaw muscles twitched. His mouth was tight as a knife blade. His voice shook. *"Loco, I'm very near to scalping you!"* As he spoke his eyes became slits. His hand went down to the Boy Scout knife scabbarded on his belt.

"OK, OK," I said. "Loco speaks with forked tongue." I think it helped saying, "forked tongue" because the red in his neck went from bloody red to faint pink. The hand on the knife reached into a leather satchel that hung from his left shoulder. He took out a pipe. It was beautiful. The bowl was small and simple. It was made of red stone. The wooden stem was as long as my forearm; two Red Bird wings, tied to a short leather strap, hung from the stem.

He took the satchel off, laid it on the ground, placed the pipe on it and said, "This is our war pipe. It will give us power. Now, the White Eyes have come. They spread across our land like locusts. They kill us. We will not let this happen, for we are Apaches. After we have smoked the pipe we will drive them back. Follow me. I will paint your faces for war. I will sharpen your weapons. I will gather horses an' guns. Then, they cannot stand against us."

At that moment, as the words came from his mouth, Billy Bob turned fully into Geronimo. As he called us to join him in driving the White Eyes from our land we answered with war whoops.

We were barefoot and wearing only shorts in front of which we had tucked white dishtowels so that they hung down like breechclouts. In those days, in the summer, the bottoms of kids' feet were tough as horses' hooves. We all had red bandanas tied around our foreheads.

Billy Bob pulled a black and white photograph from the satchel and held it up. We leaned forward. There were five Indians in a line: one was a baby; the other four were men; two of the men were in the center on horseback. "I'm the cruel lookin' one on the horse with a blaze. See those white stripes across their noses an' cheeks? That's lightnin'. Cochise gimme the paint." TC handed him the tube of toothpaste. "Now, I'm goin' to get ya'll ready for war. Chatto, lean over toward me."

One at a time, Billy Bob put a streak of white toothpaste across our faces. When he finished, we looked at one another. "Hell, Billy...I mean Geronimo, that's not half bad." said Double M. As he talked he squnched his face up trying to look mean. "How do I look?"

"Bad...real bad, like a Cherry...What is it we are?" asked Bush.

"*CHIRICHAUA!* Can't ya'll remember anything?" slashed Billy Bob.

I looked around. Everyone's face had hardened; our hair was longer and black; mouths were thin lines; eyes showed no mercy; skins were dark and tough as leather; we were transformed by another of Billy Bob's heroic visions. But, more had to happen before we swept down out of the hills without warning to raid the unsuspecting ranchers. There were more ceremonies to perform: the sharing of blood... and the smoking of the war pipe.

"Chirichauas, you are my people. We are of one blood!" As Billy Bob spoke he pulled the knife from the scabbard, touched its point to his thumb; then, in a voice I had never heard before, except in movies when something serious was about to happen, something so serious it made you hold your breath, he said, "We will share our blood." And with that he began making a small cut on his thumb and then on the others each time pressing his thumb against theirs.

When he came to me I looked away as he cut my thumb. Then I fainted. I fell over sideways. Someone splashed water on my face and pulled me upright.

I shook my head. "Damn, that hurt like a son-of-a-bitch." But I was proud. We had mixed our blood. Truly, we were now "Blood Brothers."

Then, Billy Bob bowed his head to the pipe and picked it up with both hands and raised it up to the sun. "Sun Father, bless your sacred war pipe. We will breathe its breath in and blow it upward to you.... Chatto, give me the sacred tobacco." Double M handed the five cigarettes over and Billy Bob slit the paper with his knife and one after the other pushed the tobacco down into the bowl. When he finished he held the pipe toward the sun. "Now Chatto, give me the sacred fire." Double M reached in the pocket of his shorts and took out two wooden kitchen matches and handed them to Billy Bob. We watched in silence. He lit a match, put it to the bowl and took three deep breaths. Immediately, smoke rose. He turned slowly and blew smoke in the six directions.

He passed the pipe around the circle; each of us blew smoke toward the sun. It came to me. I have asthma. I took a deep breath. For a second I thought I was going to pass out again. I coughed hard enough for my insides to come out. Bush began to pound my back; TC took a slug of water from his canteen and spit in my face.

Billy Bob Geronimo looked at me with disgust. We were no longer boys playing a game. We were Apache warriors following our leader, the great Geronimo. *We were the rulers of our world.* Geronimo rose on his toes, "Hear me now. All this land an' all that is in it is ours. Today, we will sweep across it. First, we must take up our weapons. They are in the 'Sacred Wickiup'. I will bring them to you an' place them in your hands."

He turned, bent down, and entered the low opening of an oval shaped brush hut that stood beside the "Sacred Tree." In a moment, he came out with his arms wrapped around a gosh-awful armful of what he called "weapons." Mostly they looked like a bunch of sticks. "As War Chief, I will take the largest bow, four arrows, an' one of the tomahawks." He laid the rest at his feet.

"Cochise, since you are the best shot next to me you, shall have this strong bow an' three arrows.

"Chatto, the third bow is yours with two arrows.

"Victorio, you get the longest spear an' the other tomahawk.

"Loco, this will be your spear."

"Damn, Geronimo...is that all I'm gettin'. That little thing ain't even got a point on it. It wouldn't kill a chipmunk much less a human being...Damn!"

"Well, you're the littlest an' that's all that's left."

I was about to cry. He could see it. "OK Loco, remember you're a warrior. I'll let you choose where we're going to raid."

"Really...Me?"

"Yeh."

Oh my gosh! My mind raced. Who had something we wanted? What could we get away with and not get caught and killed by our parents? Who in the neighborhood did we dislike the most? Who did I dislike the most? The words jumped from my mouth.

"BROTHER BLACK!"

A few weeks before, Brother Black, a Church of Christ preacher, had embarrassed me terribly in front of Bush and Double M, both Catholics. TC, Billy Bob, and I were Church of Christers. We went to Lipscomb, a Church of Christ school where Brother Black taught. He knew us, especially me, since he sometimes preached at our church. Next to his house, which was only two streets away from where I lived, he owned a large field where he boarded people's horses.

On the day of my humiliation we had caught a lost pony on the Lipscomb campus and needed somewhere to keep her until we found the owner. I was certain Brother Black would help us out so I volunteered to go to the front door and ask him. Being as he was a preacher I knew he would say, "Absolutely boys, turn her loose in the field and come ride her anytime you want until you find her owner. I've got a pony saddle and bridle you can use. Is there anything else you need?"

But on that hot summer day, with a big smile on his beaming, righteous face, that Man of God looked down on us, and in his best preacher-voice said, "A dollar a day, boys, a dollar a day. That's what I charge everybody, and to be fair to everybody that's what I'll have to charge you."

I stumbled away, my head hanging down, muttering, "No, thanks...no thanks." We didn't have a dollar a week among us. Sixty-five years later, the bitter taste of that rejection remains fresh in my mouth. But on the day it happened my mind was saying as my feet drug me away, *'I'll get you back, Brother Butt Hole!'*

Now, my time had come.

"So, what's this about Brother Black?" asked Geronimo.

I jumped to my feet and shook my spear in the air. "*Ha-ya! We'll set his horses free to run with the wind. We'll take revenge on that White Eye for shaming us. Ha-ya! Blood for Blood! Ha-ya!*"

"*Well, Damn, Loco!*" Geronimo stepped back and stared at me like I was someone else. *I was.* Apache blood burned in my veins. I was ready to strike our enemy. I could see in Billy Bob's eyes that he was seeing that day again and was hearing that preacher say, *A dollar a day, boys, a dollar a day.* His eyes narrowed then expanded red with blood. He stared straight up into the sun. He seemed to grow taller and stronger. He began to stomp the ground hard, first with one foot then the other. His voice chanted—

Ha-ya Ha-ya Ha-ya Ha-ya Ha-ya
The sun's horse is a yellow stallion;
His nose, the place above his nose, is of haze,
His ears, of the small lightning, are moving back and forth,
He has come to us.

The sun's horse is a yellow stallion,
A blue stallion, a black stallion;
The sun's horse has come to us.

When he said, "The sun's horse has come to us" the first time, we came alive with his vision; we jumped to our feet and began stomping the ground, turning in circles, shaking our weapons above our heads, repeating with him the second time, "The sun's horse has come to us. We are ready. We are Apache. Hear Geronimo. He speaks!"

"Cochise, Victorio, Chatto, you will drive them toward us. Go to the far end of the pasture. Loco and I will slip up to the house to see if any White Eyes are there. If none are, I will signal you with the cry of the hawk three times: '*EEEEEEEEEE! EEEEEEEEEE! EEEEEEEEEE!*' When you hear it, climb the fence, spread out an' run screaming at the horses an' drive them toward the house. We will open the gate."

Except for the hawk screech, which was more like a girl being strangled, it sounded like a good plan.

We ran from tree trunk to tree trunk toward Brother Black's house. Both of us were now calling him "Brother Butt Hole." There was no car in the driveway or garage. Geronimo signaled me to stay behind a tree. Stooping as low as he could he ran across the lawn and peered over one windowsill after another. Then—and I couldn't believe he was doing it—he stepped up onto the front porch and knocked on the door, not once, but twice. No one came.

With that, he motioned to me and we walked out into the side yard, which sloped to the pasture below. We could see the horses—there were eleven of them. At the far end of the field was the fence where the other warriors awaited Geronimo's signal. The signal came—

"EEEEEEEEEE EEEEEEEEEE EEEEEEEEEE!"

With a final screeching scream, Geronimo began to cough, wheeze, and damn! He sounded like me having an asthma attack. I slapped him on the back. He wheeled around, "Damn you, Loco, cut that out!"

From below, we heard war cries. Running across the pasture like devils, three warriors rushed toward the grazing horses, leaping, whooping, shouting, and shaking their weapons. The horses threw their heads up, snorted, reared and wheeled in the air, and broke into a gallop straight toward us. Before they reached the slope, Geronimo threw the gate open and yelled to the top of his voice, "*Ha-ya Ha-ya Ha-ya! The sun's horse has come to us!*"

And there was another voice mixed with Geronimo's, "*Ha-ya Ha-ya Ha-ya! The sun's horse has come to us!*" At first, I couldn't tell where it was coming from then I realized it was coming from me.

Pounding the earth, the horses came pouring up the slope. In a cloud of dust they galloped through the open gate and out onto the street. Not far behind, running harder than I had ever seen them, were Cochise, Victorio, and Chatto; their faces unrecognizable with wildness; the white toothpaste melting down their cheeks, they passed me, racing behind the horses whose hooves on the asphalt street cracked like rifle shots.

We were transformed back in time and space. Our feet did not touch the earth. Our minds, our bodies enlarged with blood. No human, no animal could stop us. Like wolves we veered in and out of scrub brush, cactuses, boulders, mesas, and canyons; all was desert and air and the black stallions and blue stallions and yellow stallions blew and snorted ahead of us, their manes and tails streaming in the air behind them. We ran on and on, hollering and yelling—the horses—the Apaches—the sun—all together as one.

Then came a jolt of horns, a screeching of brakes and angry shouts. And in an instant we were all back in the real world.

All but one...

Billy Bob was standing in the middle of Granny White Pike jumping up and down and hollering, "*I was born on the prairie where the wind blows free. I was born where there were no enclosures. I was born...*" He stopped, looked around; his face flushed. He was confused, "Where am I...where is everybody?" His mouth clamped shut. For a moment he stood still as a statue, you could see reality returning horribly to him. He shuddered but didn't move from where he stood. He was lost. We looked at him...then we walked side-by-side out into the street as though the cars and horns and people and shouts were not there. We closed around our friend and leader and without a word led him across the street onto the Lipscomb campus—where the horses were now quietly grazing.

Exhausted, we plopped down on the grass near the horses. Bush and TC had their canteens. They poured water on Billy Bob's face and head. As he sputtered and cooled he gradually became himself again—almost—but not completely. His normal domineering voice and manner were completely gone. If you had not known him in the fullness of his normality you would say, 'Damn, that boy's awfully low on spunk, ain't he?' Mostly he just stared into the distance. When we asked him if he was OK he just shrugged or said a word or two so low you couldn't understand him.

Finally, TC pointed at him, "Golly, guys, look at Billy Bob's eyes, they've got that 'thousand-yard stare' just like the ones you see in soldiers eyes in *Life*. Sure as hell, he's shell-shocked. We better get him home to his mama before he starts runnin' in circles an' screamin'."

But nobody moved. We were sitting there remembering the day Billy Bob went home with his eyebrows burned off. That night's punishment was stuck in our minds forever. That night, our mothers called one another and shared their child's confession. By suppertime we had all been whipped with hands, switches, belts, and anything that didn't break bones or permanently mar flesh or soul for life.

What were we to do? Our leader had turned to mush.

And then...and then, like the Day of Judgment, Brother Black stood above us with the Wrath of God on his face. Behind him stood several men in suits who looked like God's avenging angels.

I do not want to tell you what happened to us.

The Sword in the Attic

It was 1946. The war was over. It was summer in the land of the free. School was out, the sun was shining, and not one of us—not even me—had to go to summer school. As a reward, the Lord had sent us a gift: a new street was being built a half a mile from our homes. Bulldozers were already digging up the earth, and somewhere in all that dirt hidden treasures were waiting for us—us being Bush, TC, Billy Bob, Double M, and, me. Billy Bob, our leader, was twelve. He was the oldest. I was ten and the youngest.

The day was hotter than hell; you could swim in the humid air. None of our houses had air-conditioning; as soon as we could escape from our mothers we were gone, sometimes a whole day.

We gathered with our bikes in Billy Bob's back yard. Except for our shorts, we were naked. If not for being reported to our parents by do-gooder old ladies we would have gone naked as soon as we were out of sight of our houses.

Billy Bob's freckles were growing by the hundreds everyday the sun was shining, and that was every day. Though I never breathed it aloud, I thought he looked like a colored man with some kind of gosh awful jungle disease. Double M and Bush were Catholics, which I figured was the reason their skins burned so easy. TC and I were the only ones with nice tans, me because I had some Indian blood; I don't know where TC's came from.

The new street was next to a big field where Brother Black kept horses. The summer before, Brother Black, a preacher and teacher at the Church of Christ school TC, Billy Bob and I attended had tried to beat us out of a dollar a day to keep a lost pony we'd found. All of our allowances together didn't make a dollar a day. As we walked away with the pony TC had whispered, "Scrooge." I whispered back, "He's *a tight-fisted old crap-head.*" Double M and Bush had smirks on their faces, seeing it was a blow for the side of the Catholics.

When we got to where the bulldozers had been digging we spread out and began to circle, like five sharp-eyed buzzards searching the up-turned earth for a dead rabbit, or dog, or better yet a cat. Our anticipation was probably better than anything we were likely going to find on the ground half covered with dirt. Hopeful anticipation is one of the things that helps you get up in the morning; if you don't have it, then you might as well roll over and go back to sleep. Or die.

One of the best things about living in the South is all the dead people in the ground. They are everywhere: dead Indians, dead soldiers, and just plain old dead people. Now and then, some lucky kid or archeologist will hit the jackpot; better than finding bones of dead people is finding bones of a prehistoric beast, especially something really big like a saber tooth tiger, or a giant bear, or a mastodon. Finding one of these would sure as anything get your picture in the paper and turn your playmates green with envy.

My dream was to find a stone-box grave with a complete Indian skeleton and a lot of gold jewelry, or a rusty bayonet with dried blood on it, or a rifle barrel, even a Minnie ball–anything that had killed a Yankee. It would have been better than making straight A's all year long and having a string of gold stars by your name. Finding a stone-box grave that hadn't been messed up by a dozier or a stupid grownup was the kind of thing that created such excitement that it almost made you wet your shorts or start a shoving match to see who got first bids on what was inside.

It was Saturday. No one was working. We had all the dug up earth to ourselves. The only others were a bunch of sparrows scratching and pecking. We spread out, peering and sniffing at the ground. Occasionally, someone would shout and we'd run to them, our anticipations leaping us across the stones and clods to reach the shouter and to–nothing but an old tennis shoe or an Orange Crush bottle. I thought Billy Bob was going to hit Double M with a rock when Double M hollered because a bee had stung him. Billy Bob had little sympathy for us when we were in pain. "You sissy, spit on it and quit whining," was all the compassion and medical treatment Double M was going to get.

We'd been there about an hour, getting dirtier and dirtier, and tireder and thirstier by the minute, when all of a sudden, Bush gave a shout and enough "Damns" it made us know we'd better come running, "DAMN...DOUBLE DAMN! Ya'll look what I found! DAMNATION! DAMNATION!"

We stood around him in a circle and looked down. Six inches beyond our toes we could see the top of two broad stones. In various tones, we all echoed, "DAMNATION!" as we looked down at the top of what we were certain was a stone box grave. We had seen pictures of them in books and read in newspapers about people finding them but none of us had ever seen one in real life, much less found one.

The two slabs were clearly outlined beneath a thin covering of dirt. We waited for Billy Bob's orders. He was our leader because of his fast fists, which all of us had felt at one time or another.

Finally he spoke, "Well I'll be damn!"

We all nodded.

"Well, you guys quit standin there, get down an clean it off."

On our hands and knees we worked swiftly as though he had a bullwhip cocked above us and was ready to flay our naked backs. With a quick stirring of dust up into our eyes and nostrils, it was done.

"OK, OK, get back an let me do tha liftin so nothin goes wrong."

We stood up and took a couple of steps back and watched.

He squatted at the far end of the largest stone, reached out, crooked his fingers in the crack between the two stones, took a deep breath and began to stand, pulling the stone upward. His eyes and cheeks bulged; the places where he wasn't freckled turned red and he made a strange sound, like something was boiling inside his mouth. I thought his head was going to explode and splatter all over us.

Then it happened...the stone slipped from his hands and he fell backwards into the dirt.

We watched as it fell in slow motion–down–down–down. For a second, there was silence. No one breathed. No birds sang. The clouds did not move. The heat waves stopped rising.

The end of the world will sound like the sound that was made as the stone crashed back into the grave. There was a sharp cracking of bones and pottery, and the startled flapping of sparrow's wings as they burst upward and, above these, were our cries to God for mercy.

The dust blinded us. A little more and we would have smothered to death. No one moved, not even to help Billy Bob to his feet. No one spoke. We were struck dumb. All we could feel was a dreadful fear. We were frozen in a black and white photograph of people long dead.

"Well, who'n hell's goin to help me up."

Bush and TC pulled Billy Bob to his feet.

The dust was still so thick we couldn't see into the grave.

We waited.

And waited.

Finally, the air cleared. We stepped forward and peered down into the grave. What we saw was so far beyond disbelief no word has yet been created for it. The only thing that could have done more damage to the skeleton and pottery would have been six sticks of dynamite. All that remained was dust and the crumbs of the skeleton and pottery.

There was total silence. I think Billy Bob could see inside our heads. What he saw wasn't pretty. If he had spoken we would have killed him right then and there and stuffed his body into the grave, filled it in with dirt and rocks, smoothed it over on top. And then we would have: made a pact to never tell anyone, dusted ourselves off, gotten on our bikes, and gone home for lunch.

All we got were a few teeth and finger bones. I drilled holes in mine and made a necklace I still wear sometimes on Halloween.

Ten minutes later we were at Bush's. We were starving. Mr. and Mrs. Miller, his parents, were gone for the day. Before I go on, I should explain that the world opened up to us when any of our parents were gone from home for a good part of the day. It was like going to Treasure Island. We searched our parentless houses better than the F.B.I. could have. Attics, basements, refrigerators, closets, under beds, and pretty much anything closed that wasn't chained and padlocked was ours to find, to look into, to touch, to eat and even drink—and more, much more. We saw things we were not supposed to see, some we did not understand; we discovered relatives we had not known existed, some beautiful, some who looked like gangsters; and we learned of good things and bad things that brought smiles, sniggers and silence.

In the Miller's kitchen we turned into locusts. We drank all the milk, ate a whole loaf of bread, a jar of peanut butter, a jar of grape jelly, and finished off all the cookies in the cookie jar. Then we went to the basement to the den. Bush flipped the lights on. What a den it was, with its large stone fireplace and pine paneled walls covered with photographs. The chairs and couch were covered with big cushions. But what made it the most special den I had ever seen was the bar and bar stools in the corner. On the wall, behind the bar, were three shelves filled with bottle after bottle of scotch, gin, vodka, bourbon, brandy, sherry, and stuff I'd never heard of. The rows of gleaming glasses, their sparking reflections of light and the different colors of liquor, the varied shapes of bottles and labels, and stacks of glasses, was the next thing to any decorated Christmas tree I had ever seen. We couldn't take our eyes off of it.

Before anyone else made a sound, Bush said, "Ya wanta drink?"

Bush's family, the Millers, were genetically Catholic, which leads into the world of theology, a world where people lose their tempers easily and tend to get a lot of satisfaction out of shortcomings in those who believe differently than they do.

A good example is what I knew about Catholics:

They were condemned to eat fish every Friday for eternity.

They baptized babies by sprinkling water on their heads instead of shoving them totally underwater.

They had to sit in little closets and tell awful things about themselves and then a priest they couldn't even see would give them a lot of tiring stuff to do and say.

They had to do what they were told by the Pope who couldn't even speak good English, if at all, and wore a long robe instead of a suit and tie, like grown preachers should. Also, he wanted to take over the United States.

In school the nuns beat hell out of boys' knuckles and palms.

They liked to drink and dance and gamble and have lots of children.

When they died they might have to hang around in a strange place for a long time before they ended up in heaven or hell.

They had a secret men's club called the Knights of Columbus where they took an oath to kill all kinds of people, most especially Masons. My father was a Mason.

When I'd say these things—except the part about killing—to Bush and Double M, they'd start getting offended and try to argue with me but nothing they said held any water, since

I had heard the truth direct from the mouths of preachers and teachers.

I never showed Bush or Double M my authentic copy of the oath members of the Knights of Columbus had to take. It had been passed out at school. It was long and went on and on until it finally reached the really good part:

"I do further promise and declare that I will, when opportunity presents, make and wage relentless war, secretly and openly against all heretics, Protestants and Masons...I will secretly use the poison cup, the strangulation cord, the steel of the poniard, or the leaden bullet...That I will provide myself with arms and ammunition that I may be in readiness when the word is passed, or I am commanded to defend the church either as an individual or with the militia of the Pope...

"In testimony hereof, I take this most holy and Blessed Sacrament of the Eucharist and witness the same further with my name written with the point of this dagger dipped in my own blood and seal in the face of this Holy Sacrament."

Well there it was in black and white. The first time I read it, it scared me so bad I dreamed that night about Mr. Miller strangling my father with a green and gold cord. I never showed the oath to anyone, especially my parents; I kept it hidden in the bottom of the cardboard box that held my comic books. I think I was afraid if my parents saw it, especially my father, it would somehow make it come true and would result in him being poisoned, or strangled, or run through with a dagger.

And it was going to be done by Mr. Miller. He was one of them. He was a member of the Knights of Columbus. The year before I was given the copy of the oath, Mr. Miller had taken Bush and me with him to the Knights of Columbus white, two-story building; right up the steps and in the front door and then through another door that opened into a high-ceilinged room, the size of a basketball court. He spoke to everybody and they spoke to him. They all seemed to be friends. They all called him "Johnny."

My eyes stretched as wide as they could go. The room they called 'The Hall', was a wonder to behold: slot machines, pinball machines, roulette tables, card tables, and crap tables were everywhere. On the walls were paintings of men wearing dark blue robes and feathered hats, several with swords. Above the paintings, flagpoles slanted outward, some with American flags; others were gold and blue with green crosses on them. From the rafters hung blue banners with gold lettering, many with the symbol of an ax head, sword, and what looked like an anchor. At the far end, above the fireplace, were two crossed swords with silver blades and golden handles. Through an open door, I could see a dimly lit room with a bar and tables where men were drinking and laughing. But what made me really stop and stare were two priests: one shooting dice, the other spinning a roulette wheel.

I remember little else, not even how long we were there. The strangeness of it scared me a little and I moved closer to Mr. Miller; yet there was a part of me, a large part of me, thrilled by it all.

Mr. Miller loved beer—Miller beer. He traveled all across middle Tennessee as a newspaper distributor. In the summer, he often took Bush and me with him. Every day, at lunchtime, he would take us to the best place, in whatever town we were in, that served good hamburgers, french fries and ice-cold beer. He always drank draft beer in a mug bigger than a soup bowl. Sitting across from him, I could hardly take my eyes off the white foam above the amber beer and the icy skim on the mug. It looked almost as good as a chocolate milkshake. When he drank, it made a white streak above his upper lip like a mustache, and when he salted it the foam rose like magic. He was a good man who liked to: tease me, laugh, and tousle my hair. He and Mrs. Miller and all their family were always kind, treating me as one of them. It was from them and from my parents I eventually learned that kindness can be greater than a lie and that, sometimes, kindness is even greater than religion. But that day had not yet come when I was ten years old.

"Well, do ya'll wanta drink?"

The words had barely gotten out of Bush's mouth the second time when we all shouted, "YES!"

"OK," he said, "Wait a minute." He ran from the room and up the steps and was back in an instant with an empty coke bottle filled with water and a funnel and towel. "I'll be tha bartender an do tha mixin, since it's my liquor an my bar."

With that, he turned and took down every open bottle. There were seven of them. Next, he got a tall glass and poured maybe four or five thimble-fulls from each bottle into the glass. After the seventh bottle, he put the funnel in its mouth and replaced the exact amount taken out with water, put the top back on, wiped the bottle off, shook it a little and placed it back in its exact place on the shelf. He repeated this seven times; totally concentrated on his concoction, he never looked up, never said a word. It was like watching a movie of a great scientist in his laboratory turning out a cure for Billy Bob's jungle disease. We were in awe. I knew of no Church of Christ boy who had anywhere near this kind of genius. He was so good at it, it made think he had done it before.

After the last bottle was back on the shelf, he took a spoon from under the bar and briskly stirred everything together. He held the glass close to his eyes. When it was mixed to his satisfaction he looked up and said, "What'll we call it?

Billy Bob said, "How bout 'Witches' Brew'," which didn't have any imagination at all.

"Or 'Vampire Blood'," said TC who, still wet his bed after seeing a Bela Lugosi or Lon Chaney movie.

"Or, how bout 'Seven Farts to tha Wind'," said Double M who had a thing about saying farts, and was always trying to work the word in no matter how inappropriate it was.

The night before, I'd been to the movies with my parents. We'd seen a John Wayne war film that had left me feeling patriotic on the inside, "No you guys, they ain't any good. Since we just beat the hell out of the Germans an Japs lets call it the, 'Victory Drink'."

The others squnched their noses up and turned their thumbs down.

Then, with finality, Bush spoke, "Look you guys, since I made it and I'm the bartender, I'll name it. I once heard my daddy say the name of a drink that beats tha hell outa any thing ya'll have come up with...It's a 'Singapore Sling'."

So it was named.

"OK Bush," said Billy Bob, "Since you named it, how bout you goin upstairs an gettin some cigarettes for us to smoke with it."

Immediately, we all backed Billy Bob with our; "Unhuhs."

It was clear Bush didn't like it, but he got up and went back upstairs. This time he was gone longer. When he came back, he held his hand out and opened it; there were four half cigarettes and one whole one which he immediately put in his mouth, "The halves are yours, take it or leave it!"

We took our halves, then we all lit up and Bush poured the drinks, about four tablespoons each. With that, we sat down on the soft cushions, leaned back, and, like soldiers of fortune in a Bogart film, smoked our cigarettes and sipped our martinis.

Ten seconds later: coughs, gags, hacking, red faces, and a lot of "Damns" filled the room. And the Bogart film ground to a halt.

When we finished spitting into the bar's sink we got some soap and washed our mouths out, to remove the slightest trace of Singapore Sling. We smelled each other's breaths until we were certain our mothers could not pick up the slightest scent of our sin. To get Billy Bob back for destroying our skeleton, Bush and I told him we could still smell a little alcohol on his breath, so he should wash his mouth a second time.

In our church, drinking alcohol was right up there with murder, fornication, mixed swimming, and dancing. It could send you straight to hell. Billy Bob, TC, and I didn't have one of those places like Bush and Double M had where you could hang around for a while—we just went straight on to hell. Of course, all of us were going to end up in hell on earth if our mothers found out we'd been drinking and smoking.

After we'd cleaned up all the traces of our binge, we still had a couple of hours before the Millers returned home. We went to the second floor and began to systematically look in all the drawers and closets, with particular attention given to the room of Bush's older sister.

We saved the attic for last. It was narrow and long and smelled of mothballs. It was full of stuff: winter clothes, Christmas decorations, boxes of cards, letters and photographs, luggage, and more boxes on top of boxes.

Halfway into the attic, a glint of light above me caught my eye. I looked up. Two shelves ran the length of the right side of the room. On the highest shelf I could see the edge of a silver strip of metal. I pointed to it, "Bush, what's that?"

He looked and in a rather off-handed tone said, "O that, that's my father's Knights of Columbus sword."

I almost fainted, *O my God, that's what Mr. Miller is going to use to cut my daddy's head off with.* I could feel my left eyelid twitching; all my breath caught in my throat; I might not breath or speak again.

Bush turned around and looked at me, "What's wrong with you? Are you sick? You better not vomit in here."

Billy Bob punched me in the back. It hurt like hell but started me to breathing and talking again, "Can I see the sword?"

"Yeah, but you got to swear on your mother's grave not to vomit."

"I swear on her grave." I said.

Bush looked at Billy Bob, "Can you reach it?"

Billy Bob was a full head taller than me. He was the tallest of all of us and lean as a beanpole. He stood on his toes, stretched his long arms and fingers; all of him was just enough to reach the sword's scabbard and lift it down.

Bush took it from him, gripped the handle, pulled the sword from its scabbard, and held the blade up to the ceiling light. It glistened like Excalibur.

The second I saw it, I knew it could cut my father's head off. It was long, silvery, and sharper than hell. I wanted to hold it. But before I could ask, Bush slid the sword back into the scabbard and gave it to Billy Bob, who put it back on the shelf.

Then, it was time to go home.

As the years passed we went our separate ways. The Millers moved away first, then TC and his family. After Billy Bob and Double M graduated from high school and went off to college, we might run into each other ever year or so. We'd talk a few minutes and make promises to get together and bring each other up to date. We never did. I made new friends, as I'm sure they did. Slowly I forgot them. But then, a few years back, when I started writing they suddenly came into my mind. I wrote a story about the five of us called *Pony*, followed by *Ride To Glory* and *Would You Give An Eye To See A...?* and now, as I write *The Sword In The Attic*, I see us clearly again: half naked, sitting around our 'Cussin Tree', smoking and telling our newest dirty jokes, driving our soap-box racers through cardboard walls of fire, riding the lost pony that was the color of pure gold, and I hear our laughter and 'Damnations' as we shoot one another on our bare backs with rubber-guns, and, for a little, while we are together again.

WOULD YOU GIVE AN EYE TO SEE A…?

It was our very last Friday before the end of summer vacation: our last three days of freedom, our last three days before we returned to the fiery pit, our last three days before our parents forced us back to school.

There were five of us. Billy Bob was twelve and the oldest. He had fast fists and was our leader. TC, Bush, and Double M were eleven. I was ten, the youngest, and the follower. Bush and Double M were Catholic, the rest of us Church of Christ.

We were sprawled on the ground beneath the 'Cussin Tree.' Hidden from the spying eyes of grown ups by wild hedges and bushes, it's where we went to smoke and talk ugly and plot and scheme against the unfair rules of grownups. It's also where we learned from one another some of the facts of life, wonderfully distorted though they so often were. We'd just finished a close examination of the Women's Underwear section in the Sears Roebuck Catalogue I had brought, and were smoking away on the Camels Billy Bob had confiscated from his father. Everyone's face was serious.

"Well, we'd better make tha best outta tomorrow," said Bush.

"Damn right bout that," said TC.

"Double damn right bout that," said Double M.

"Well we better come up with somethin good, cause ya'll know what comes after tomorrow," I said.

Except for school days, Sunday mornings were the most horrible part of the week. God could have done a whole lot better when He made it. Every Sunday morning we had to pay for our sins of smoking, lying, stealing, cursing, and for—well you know—what boys do at night under the covers. Penance began with scrubbed faces, slicked down hair, starched shirts, itchy suits, and ties so tight they could have strangled a Silverback Gorilla to death.

Church was ninety percent boredom and ten percent pure terror. Most preachers weren't worth a tinker's damn when it came to holding a kid's attention. But it's sort of funny, for the older I've gotten the more appreciation I've had for all those years of being bored to death in church. I think it helped me out in life. During the half an hour the preacher was droning on and on, I would sit there dreaming up all kinds of stuff in my head that might keep me out of school for a few days: things like breathing in a lot of dust and having an attack of asthma, or drinking enough soapy water to make myself vomit, or getting a dog to bite me. Church was a hothouse that helped my imagination grow.

Then there were those ten percent times of terror. These were usually during revivals. Revivals were held at least once a year, more often if the elders thought the congregation's attention wasn't focused enough on the Final Judgment or that the numbers were slipping on baptisms and restorations. They'd bring in some fire-and-brimstone big name that could scare the daylights out of adults and terrorize the children. He'd get so worked up you could taste sulfur in the air and see the Devil's face reflecting in his eyes.

Sometimes I couldn't look, I'd get so scared. A couple of times I wet my bed at night.

My preference was stories from the Old Testament; those were filled with throwing people to lions, walls of water drowning millions of Egyptians, dogs eating women, and Samson killing a ton of Philistines with the jawbone of an ass. These kept me wide-awake with my eyes and ears glued on the preacher. But I paid for it at night. The sounds and pictures of all that screaming and blood and death would creep into my bedroom and scare me so bad I'd cover my head with the sheet and pray out loud until I fell asleep. I think these gory sermons influenced my later love of horror stories and movies and some of my own gory writings. So church wasn't entirely wasted on me.

Thank the good Lord my family was Church of Christ. If they'd been Catholic I would have been dead before I was eight years old. I had asthma. Breathing all that smoke pouring out of those little buckets the priests swung around and around over everybody's head would have sure as anything smothered me to death right there in my pew. And as to being an alter boy—un uh—dressing up like a girl in a long white gown and carrying big, tall things and chanting in Latin would have been worse than what I up against in church.

Speaking of Latin, I need to say something about its affect on my life. I tried it out for two years in high school and for two years it gave me a splitting headache. I suffered just like the saying goes, "Latin is a dead language, as dead as can be. First, it killed the Romans, now it's killing me." It would have been easier on my brains to have pounded my head against a rock as against Caesar's *Gallic Wars*. I made two years of straight Ds. When I reminded Ms. Whitten, my

Latin teacher, of this at our fiftieth high school reunion she tried to reassure me with the comforting words, "But George, they were all good Ds."

So there we were under the Cussin Tree trying to come up with a good plan for living it up on Saturday. One dumb idea after another had been shot down when TC, who was leaning back on his elbows, sat up, took a deep draw off his cigarette and said, "I'll tell you what we outta do, there's a double feature at tha Princes an they're showing *Strangler Of The Swamp* and *Isle Of The Dead* with Boris Karloff...Man, ya can't beat Karloff for our last day on earth together." TC, was prone to speak in extremes and loved horror movies more than he loved his little sister. He saw he had our attention. He took another deep draw, paused dramatically, looked slowly around at each of us, then said, "Hell, ya'll know there's only one place for us to go...we gotta spend tha whole day downtown."

While he wasn't known for having good ideas, the moment TC said it we all knew he had knocked the ball out of the park. Downtown it was!

Downtown Nashville was our playground and one of our schools of life. We roamed it. We explored it. We tasted and smelled it. Nooks and crannies, every alley, every stairwell, every rooftop held something new; at times something disturbingly glorious and—now and then—we discovered something so horrible it returned in the dark of the night, hovering above our beds. The city was filled with blind musicians, beggars, all shades of colored people, parades of women with mink around their shoulders, men in pin-striped suits and two-toned shoes, and a man without legs rolling down the sidewalk on a small wooden shelf attached to roller-skates.

If we didn't ride the bus to town, my father would drive us in one of his shiny Cadillacs to his car lot on Broad, two blocks from the heart of downtown. None of the other fathers had cars approaching anywhere near my dad's Cadillacs. He was a man to behold. He was big and prosperous looking. He wore a diamond ring. His fingernails were polished. His hair was oiled and slicked back; his suits, shirts, ties, and shiny shoes were the finest and always immaculate. I took some pride in having a father who could have passed for a gangster where none of the other fathers could have. From his lot we headed into the heart of the city like a small band of Cherokee searching and hunting for whatever prey was unfortunate enough to cross our path.

First and foremost was Harveys, Nashville's largest and newest Department Store. It had everything: real live monkeys in a cage beside a soda fountain, a carousel, clowns, and, most special of all, the city's first escalators. Six floors high, we could spend a good couple of hours there playing hide-and-go-seek, cramming all five of our bodies into elevators filled with the bodies of women shoppers, examining naked female mannequins and women's lingerie, and running up the escalators going down and down those going up.

From Harveys, we advanced, side-by-side, up the sidewalk to the State Museum beneath the War Memorial building. The Museum contained two of Tennessee's greatest possessions: big glass jars of formaldehyde with things in them—horrible things—that looked like babies; the other was an Egyptian mummy that was just a little older than our grandparents.

We could hardly take our eyes off the things floating in the jars.

Bush whispered, “Oh my gosh, are those real babies?”

“You dummy!” said TC, “Can’t you see they ain’t babies, they’re aliens. I saw some that looked just like em in *Monsters From Mars.* My dad says they’re everywhere out in New Mexico. Flying Saucers land out there all tha time an my dad says that tha government keeps it a big secret. These must have been some that got away an got run over on the highway an somebody from Tennessee found em and picked em up an contributed em to the Museum. Hell, they might even have come from somewhere up in tha Smokies. I bet they land up there too.”

“Oh my gosh! I ain’t ever goin to tha Smokies again.”

“Yep, that’s exactly what they are. They’re aliens!”

Bush was beginning to look a little queasy, like he might throw up. I guess he would have if Billy Bob hadn’t brought us back down to earth with a sharp finality, “Hells-fire-an-damnation ya’ll, let’s go look at tha mummy.”

The mummy mesmerized Billy Bob. I believe he would have skipped going to a movie or eating Krystals just to stand there and stare at it—especially where its sex parts were, or at least where they should have been; as far as I could tell whatever had been there a million years before had dried up and fallen off. Every time he looked at it, his eyes would bulge and start shining and his face would turn red and now and then his body would quiver and every time he’d say the same thing, “Ya’ll, look-a-there. Look-a-there. Look at his weenie. Look at his weenie!” And he’d be pointing with his finger and it would be jerking back and forth like it was going straight through the glass.

His voice would rise higher and higher and we’d tell him to hush up or a guard would come in. And one time one did. He stared at us for a minute then asked, “What’s goin on here?" We were so scared nobody answered. I could see he was studying Billy Bob the hardest. I think he figured it all out quickly because he stuck his thumbs in his gun belt and nodded toward Billy Bob, "OK, you fellows get on outa here right now an be sure an take him with you. We don't want his type hangin around here." Double M and Bush got behind Billy Bob and shoved him ahead of us until we got outside. Once the sun and air hit him he began to come back.

Next stop was the State Capitol. While not quite as good as the Museum, it had its points. There was a real dead man named William Strickland in its walls. First thing we'd do was go to the exact spot where his bones or whatever was in there, and put our ears up against the stone to see if we could hear anything. Then we'd put our hands on the stone to see if it was cooler than the others, for that was a sure sign a ghost or spirit was there.

Though horror movies sometimes made TC wet his bed, he loved Poe as much as he loved Count Dracula and Frankenstein movies. Before he said it, I knew exactly what was going to come out of his mouth because I'd read everything Poe had written.

"I betcha he was buried alive in there!"

Double M leaned forward and put his ear against the stone. All of us held our breaths and watched. For a minute nothing happened then, his lips stretched away from his teeth, his eyes bulged, his face contorted, and a guttural rasping came from deep in his throat. Bush was standing right beside me; I heard a faint voice, almost as though it had no breath, "Oh my gosh...Oh my gosh...that thing's in there an it's alive..."

Just as Bush said, "that thing's in there an it's alive," Double M shoved back away from the wall, leaped into the air with his face like a madman's, his hands like claws and screeched, "*YAAEEEeeeeee!*"

It scared me so bad I squnched my eyes and covered my face with my hands.

Then he began laughing loudly and I heard a 'thud.'

"Damn, that hurt!" cried Double M.

"Well that's for you bein a damn fool," said Billy Bob.

I took my hands away and opened my eyes.

Double M was rubbing his right shoulder where Billy Bob had hit him. TC was rising from a crouch where he had folded his arms over his head for protection. Bush was nowhere to be seen.

Ten minutes later we found him hiding in the Men's Restroom. For a bit he refused to come out of the stall. It took all of us to convince him that it was just another of Double M's sick jokes. Finally the stall door opened slowly and Bush peeked out. He looked both ways, seeing there was no moldy dead man in the room he stepped out. Glaring at Double M, he hissed, "You're sick," and walked out of the restroom.

Before we left the Capitol we went inside and took a quick look at the chipped place on the marble handrail beside the wide steps that led up to the Senate and House Chambers; the crack was made by one politician shooting at another and missing. Every time we stuck our fingers in the crack we were disappointed no one had been killed.

From the Capitol we descended upon the Bennie Dillon building; it was twelve stories high. There were two things that drew us to that building every time we were downtown: the stairwell and the rooftop.

From the top floor of the stairwell was a ten-inch opening between the handrails all the way down to the ground floor. From the top floor you could see hands on the railing as people came up the steps. The goal was to spit and hit the hand. Nine out of ten times we missed but on the tenth, when you struck your target and heard the horrified scream of a woman or the loud cursing of a man, it was better than making an A in Latin. Because of my asthma and congestion I tended to have several gallons more mucous than the others, thereby I was, hands down, the champion spitter—it was usually my spit that hit.

If you hit a man as old as Methuselah or one with a bad leg all you'd get was a lot of ugly language, but if you hit a man who could still run up steps the next thing you'd hear was pounding footfalls as he came tearing upward shouting, "When I catch you I'm going to rip your mouth out then I'm going to kill you."

Then, like Bush at the Capital, we would flee to the nearest restroom and hide in the stalls, even if we all had to cram into one. There we waited: not breathing, not talking, praying silently; after a half a day or so, if it was quiet, we'd send the one who'd hit the hand out to see if the assassin was gone. If so, we'd go back and spit awhile more until our spit ran out. Then we would go to the rooftop.

We knew almost every unoccupied part of the Bennie Dillon Building. The rooftop was the most special spot of all. From there you could see the river and barges, the distant tree-covered hills; leaning over the low brick wall at the edge you could see the shoppers—they scurried back and forth like ants, in and out of holes, twisting their antennas, telling one another where they had just bought this or that, or had just eaten that or this, and then they scurried on to other holes and other ants.

As there was a strong desire within me to live, I was terrified about standing anywhere near the edge of anything over twelve feet high. Twelve stories into the sky was the next thing to being on Everest without any ropes around you. The nearer I got to the edge of the rooftop the more my imagination took hold. A malignant force drew me forward. To avoid being called 'chicken,' I would ease up to it, barely lifting my feet, and look over the side then quickly step back. In that one glance down through the clouds to the earth far below, I could see myself toppling over that little bitty, frail wall and screaming for thirty minutes before I hit the sidewalk. And I could hear my dear mother weeping and see my father shaking his head at the stupidity of his idiot son.

Billy Bob was in the lead as we climbed the last steps to the door that opened onto the roof. As he put his hand on the knob he turned and looked at me, "Well Spain, are you going to jump this time?" He, like the rest of us, had a twisted sense of humor. The others laughed. I looked at my feet as Billy Bob's hand turned the knob and the door began to open.

At this point, I need to pause and explain about a game we played at the Cussin Tree. We'd be lying on the ground around it, leaning back on our elbows, smoking and telling dirty jokes when all of a sudden one of us would say, "Hey ya'll, would you give an eye to see a...?" and then he'd say something so gross or obscene it can't be repeated here; if it was really awful we'd hold our noses and make gagging sounds. But if it was something so sexually graphic we could see it; we'd sit up and lean toward the speaker with our eyes stretched wide and excited and begin to talk all at once, "My gosh, say that all over again...Damnation that's, that's...Oh my, Oh my...Do you know anymore like that?" When you got that reaction you were hands down the gross subject champion for the day! And for certain, someone would say, "Well, I'd give an eye to see that."

Billy Bob pushed the door all the way open and, one-by-one, we stepped out into the bright sunlight. For a moment we couldn't see a thing and then, suddenly, we could see. '*Oh my goodness! Oh my goodness!*' was all my mind could say. My entire body filled with electricity. If souls can quiver I think mine quivered so hard it left my body.

For a boy—and a thousand times more for a man—there's nothing God placed on this earth that comes anywhere near equaling the body of a woman who is almost naked. It is absolutely why the words 'frenzied anticipation' were created. All we hoped for. All we prayed for. Our very reason for existing.

There before us, stretched out on a towel, was a woman sun bathing in her underwear.

I clamped my hands over my eyes so fast and hard I almost broke my nose. I stopped breathing. Time passed. There was a great silence. More time passed. And then I heard my voice speak to me in my head, '*Would you give an eye to see an almost naked woman?*' There was not the slightest hint of a pause as my voice answered, '*Yes! Oh yes!*' And as it spoke I said a quick prayer, opened my left eye...and peeped between my fingers.

Long years have passed since that glorious day of sunshine and still I quiver in frenzied anticipation when I see an almost naked woman with my two good eyes. Thank you God for your never-ending mercies!

WOLF SKIN

IV Criteria Lycanthropy is thought to be a cultural manifestation of schizophrenia due to the first 4 symptomatic criteria. The first are delusions, and this fits clinical lycanthropy because a person believing that he or she turns into an animal is a delusion. The second symptom is hallucinations, and people with clinical lycanthropy have hallucinations of being an animal, and having whatever traits that animal has, whether it be claws, fur, fangs, or whatever that particular animal has. The next symptom is disorganized speech, from a...cultural perspective. [These] people, often take on the sounds of the animal they believe they turn into. So, if a person believes that he or she are a werewolf, they may begin to howl at the moon or sometimes even in the daylight. The last symptom that matches schizophrenia is grossly disorganized behavior. This is appropriate because individuals with clinical lycanthropy often act like the animal they have become, including living outside and picking up their diet.

Wikipedia

How could I have loved my mother so much after all she did? But I did love her more than anyone or anything in my life. I worshipped her, and still do, even though I now wonder if she was my mother—if I am from her egg or blood.

On the library wall, behind the desk where I am writing, hangs a Russian, she-wolf skin; six feet, nine inches long. It is beautiful. When she was killed she weighed 190 pounds.

The overall color is tawny or rufous gray, the head, back to the neck, shoulders, loins, and hindquarters are blackish with yellow tints. There is a very dense brown under fur intermixed with white and black hairs. The thighs and outer the legs are reddish yellow; the tail is dark brown above and lighter below and tipped with black; the mask is a mix of white and dark brown covered with short velvety fur with black whiskers. It glows, as though alive.

A few days from now I will be eighty. I have never married. Have no children. No brother or sister. My few cousins are near death; long ago they stopped talking to me. I practiced psychiatry for twenty years then, founded an investment company, which made me wealthy. But in recent years my wealth has been greatly reduced by the plunge in oil prices and the stock market. Wealth once gave me great satisfaction. No more. My fortune, which exceeded $300,000,000, has been cut to far less than a third of that; the stupidity of my financial advisers and bankers have brought this about. Their names and home addresses are on a list in the top drawer of my desk.

There are times, when the moon is full I only see darkness in myself. As I near the end of my life I have an overpowering need to reveal the darkness and secrets I've never told anyone; not even my analyst. They are obsessions filling my dreams, nightmares returning over and over; demons and fantasies, of beliefs and disbeliefs and lusts and obsessions that often control me at night, things that I hope this telling will cast out. If not, Freud was a "Fool" and psychoanalysis is no more than babble.

How strange I use the word "demons" for I do not believe in them as I do not believe in a god or devil. After I die there will be no soul left behind to mark my passing, only my journal, which will be published by my attorney. It will tell of the horror that has been within me since I was a boy; horror that has prevented me from ever loving another—except for my mother. I've tried to control it with mental tricks and the many pills I eat. They have all failed, even foolish incantations and fasts have not removed the pain and demons tearing and howling in me. You may understand why when you have read my story.

My mother had a dog named, "Ulf."

But...I'm getting ahead of myself.

Let me start again...start before I was born...start with my parents.

This is what my mother told me, but like many things she said it may not be true, "Our people were little more than serfs for generations; we lived and died on the lands of the Duke of Bavaria whose family had owned tens of thousands of sections stretching for miles across the valleys and mountains. Reichsburg, his castle, stood at the top of one of the Utersberg Mountains that surrounded the small town of Berchtesgaden. Your father was the Duke's head Gamekeeper. I was a healer. You were born in 1936. You were our only child."

I see her, the night of my seventh birthday, crushing herbs into a clay bowl, rubbing the pulp into the wolf skin; she suddenly looks up and says, "You are old enough now to hear how your father died; he was killed by a wolf. He had killed hundreds of them and never been hurt, not even scratched, but in the winter of 1938, two years after you were born, he was killed by a huge, Russian, she-wolf." She put her hands on the skin. "This is hers; I have kept it is as fresh as when she was killed." She leaned her face into it and did not speak again.

The next night she continued, "Your father had gone into the mountains, to 'The High Forest,' to hunt a wolf that was killing the Duke's cattle. Neither he, nor his three wolfhounds, returned." She suddenly paused and said something strange, " I am a Jew. Your father wasn't. I hated Hitler and the Nazis. We were...we are Jews...Hitler was a wolf. The Germans followed him like sheep. The Nazis killed most of my aunts and uncles and cousins. They would have killed us if we hadn't gotten away." I did not understand who Hitler and the Nazis were.

She continued, "The party searching for your father followed the trail through the snow into early afternoon. The snow had stopped. The tracks led into the forest. Ahead, they heard loud crackling and squawking of crows coming through the trees. As they came into a small glade the air was filled with crows flaring up from a slaughter pen of blood.

"The wolf was feeding on your father. They shot her nine times.

"They brought your father's body back and the skin of the wolf that had killed him. They gave the skin to me. Two days later, we buried your father in the section of the Duke's cemetery where his favorite gamekeepers were buried.

"That night I began to scrape and clean the skin. Then when I finished, I salted it and hung it on the side of our house to cure. When it was ready I took it down and began to rub pulp from plants and herbs and animal grease into it—to keep it alive. When it was ready I took the money I had saved and hidden in the cellar and fled with you to Switzerland, then to the United States, then to the south where land was cheap."

Our house was a rough-framed, wood-shingled cabin in the middle of the mountains, a few miles south of Sewanee, Tennessee. It sat on the side of a steep ravine that sloped to Crow Creek, which flowed from Buggytop Cave to the village of Sherwood and beyond. Covered in forest, the mountains around us were like a wall across the southern border of the state.

The people were poor, hard working, mostly good, decent people. All but a few accepted my mother because she could heal them and bring their babies into the world alive—but a few, like the Dorton twins, hated us as some of our ways were different and our speech strange to their ears—they called us "Kraut Jews" and said we should be run out of the mountains since we were "likely Hitler spies." Others called her the "Witch of Lost Cove" and swore that when the cove flooded they had seen her float across it in an eggshell.

Every night she rubbed her special oils into the skin. The hair glistened as though alive and when she stroked the fur against her face and touched it to her lips she whispered words I had never heard.

On September 28, 1939, eight days before my third birthday, the night was filled with moonlight. Objects were as clear as the black ink on this white paper I am writing my life upon. I had not been in bed long. The light from the moon coming through the single window in the loft where I slept was so bright I could not fall asleep.

Looking down from the window I saw who I thought was my mother come from the shadows of the house on all fours. She was completely covered by what seemed to be the wolf skin.

The next day, the Dorton twins, Sandy Joe and West Wild, were found lying face up beside their still at the north end of Lost Cove. Their faces were twisted in horror, their throats torn out. There was no evidence of who had killed them, no shoe or boot-prints, nothing—except for the paw prints of what the Sheriff, in the *Winchester Home Journal*, called "the gosh awfulest, biggest paw prints of a dog, or what ever it was, I'd ever seen in all my years; two of em were in blood smack-dab on Sandy Joe's chest. Whatever that thing was it must have been almost as big as a yearlin calf. I tell you one thing, we'd better get it fore it gets someone else. I'm lookin for volunteers to bring their rifles an sharpest nosed hounds an meet me in front of the Sewanee Chapel this Saturday at 9:00 AM to run down an kill that thing."

They hunted for a week up and down the mountains, all the way from Sewanee to Sherwood and beyond and never found a thing except some red and gray fox and three bobcats.

Sandy Joe and Wild West were the first ones.

It all started with their deaths.

She was stunningly beautiful, my mother was. When we had to go to Sewanee or Sherwood for supplies I could see it in men's eyes—I hated their eyes, even though I did not yet know that what I was seeing was lust.

When she talked or sang to me her voice and face were always gentle and loving, but they became sharp and hard when she spoke of those who were cruel. Tall and slender; there was strength in her body and smoothness in her movements; her tawny skin was tight; her long, soft, amber hair was streaked with gray. Standing beside her, I felt short, soft and stumpy. Though our differences were a terrible embarrassment to me I did not speak of it. Now I am like her, but for my mustache and shorter hair I could be her twin.

The night I saw her leave the house covered by what looked like the skin I climbed down the ladder and looked at her bed where she kept it. The skin was gone. I went back up to the loft and looked out the window, waiting for her return. I fell asleep.

I do not know how long I lay on the floor when I was awakened to the sound of long moaning howling. I could smell blood. In an instant I knew death was near. The sound and smell came from everywhere, from the ridges, from every side of the cabin; it filled the air above me and in me on and on until I screamed, "*MAAMA MAAMA!*"

The howling stopped. Only night birds called.

Year after year, those who were the personification of evil: child abusers, murderers of innocent people, and those who were always mean and cruel to others were either found with their throats torn out with paw prints around or on them, and there were those who disappeared. There was always a search—nothing—no animal, no human, was ever found.

My mother kept a *Farmer's Almanac* on the wall beside her bed. Dates of a full moon were circled. A day or two before those nights she became restless and paced back and forth in the yard and, now and then, she would stop and stare upward at the moon.

As the years passed I watched and listened and sniffed the air.

Slowly I began to ask questions.

Slowly I knew who she was.

Slowly she began to teach me.

In early Fall 1952, I left the mountains and entered Vanderbilt. I was sixteen. I had full scholarships for academics and room and board. While I knew that, except for my mother, I was more intelligent than anyone I had grown up with, I thought that at college and later, in medical school and later, in psychiatry I would begin to meet professors and colleagues as intelligent as I was. But there was not one.

When I left home my mother gave me the skin "for protection."

A week and a half later, the Franklin County Sheriff called to tell me my mother's body had been found by University students inside Buggytop cave. She was dead and our house was burned to the ground. I said nothing for a moment, then in a shocked voice, "O my God what"...I choked with a sob. "My mother is dead?"

"I'm fraid so son, an I'm so sorry." When he heard what sounded like sobbing he asked in a soft voice, "Son, I need to tell ya we had to go ahead an bury her cause of tha way we found her...she'd been hurt bad an had been dead for several days...I'm so sorry. Any thing I can do for ya here. When'll ya be home?"

I waited—thinking—before I answered. Then, "Sir, I...I think my mother would want me to stay here and come home during a break...I'd most likely loose my scholarships if I came home now and that would kill her she was so proud of me getting into Vanderbilt. 'Don't you dare come home stay there and make me proud.' That's what she would be telling you and me."

I stayed and never went back. I had all I needed from those mountains—and my mother.

In ten years, I finished college, medical school, Residency, had my license to practice medicine and psychiatry and eventually was hired as Assistant Professor by the Vanderbilt Department of Psychiatry and began to treat the mentally ill. More than ever, my mother would have been proud of all I had achieved.

It wasn't long before my reputation in the treatment of schizophrenia was known nationally. My writings for medical journals were highly regarded and I began to receive million dollar grants for research.

Within the next twelve years I was elected President of the American Psychiatric Association and was the leading researcher into the genetic causes of schizophrenia and started what was to become to one of the largest investment companies in the South.

From the beginning there have been those who opposed me: stupid, jealous, narrow-minded adversaries, some powerful, some mere fleas, who threatened me, and the success of my achievements. None succeeded.

They have all disappeared in their different ways.

The light of the full moon streaming through the open window shines on the skin. It glistens. Following my mother's instructions I have continued to rub the salve into it every night I am here. It always feels alive and ready.

I stroke my face against the fur and whisper the words she taught me. I reach up, take the skin down, turn, open the top drawer of my desk, and take the list out.

DEAD BIRD:
A DARK TALE OF FALCONRY

A hawk, flying across a field, straight at you, with its talons sinking into your glove, is beyond wonderful!

But, that was not happening today.

I'd called and cursed 'til I was hoarse, causing my dog, Lassie, to go back to the house.

No matter what I did, the damn bird would not come down to me from the damn tree.

She looked down with distain, then away.

A sky was a clear summer, Sunday afternoon, an absolutely stunning day.

We were in the front field of our small farm; fronted by a one-lane gravel road.

Trees canopied the road; a narrow creek ran beside it.

"Hawk" sat thirty feet up on the limb of a walnut tree.

She was beautiful sitting there but, she wouldn't come.

"*Hawk! Hawk! Hawk! Hawk!*"

I shouted and shouted that stupid name across the field and held my glove up.

She ruffled her feathers and looked away.

She was not hungry, not sharp-set.

"*Dad blast it!*"

I reached into the bag hanging over my right shoulder and pulled a dead starling out.

I held it in my thick falconer's glove, on my left hand, and began to pluck it.

Plucking a dead bird, shaking it, throwing it to the ground, sometimes worked.

I was a falconer by happenstance. The happenstance happened this way:

One cloudy, cold day in early November, our son, Lynch, and I were horseback riding.

He was on Natchez, a strong, red and white Appaloosa; I was on Lady, my chestnut mare.

We'd crossed the wooded hill behind our house and were headed down into a hollow.

The horse's breaths clouded the air.

We'd just reached the edge of a sage field when Natchez threw up his head and snorted.

Right in front of him a large hawk flared up.

It rose a few feet above the sage and flew erratically a short distance and went down.

We sat there watching it, "It's hurt Lynch, let's try to catch it."

We spurred our horses forward, pushing it until it finally fell to ground and did not rise.

There, against the side of a bank, it turned on its back, and stretched its talons out.

My lord, she was beautiful—a large female—her eyes fixed on mine, ready to strike.

We did not move.

I took it off my large, canvas poncho off.

She looked at me.

And I pitched it over her as she flailed away.

Bundled in my arms, across the pommel of the saddle, I rode home to our barn.

There, I dumped her into a stall that I began to pompously call, "My mews."

Her left wing was hanging down; it was dislocated.

The next day I took her to my vet who put the wing back in its socket.

Then, I went to the Nashville Public Library and took out their two books on falconry.

I was dumb as mud about hawks and birds of prey.

But slowly, "Hawk"—the name I gave her—and the books taught me.

She was a: buteo, a broad-wing hawk, a Red—tail.

I made leather straps—jesses—to go around her legs and a leash to attach to them.

I bought a pair of welder's gloves and fifty yards of nylon cord for a creance.

I put a snap-hook on the creance.

A cousin made a circular heavy-metal perch.

I had a small goatee and long hair and—by damn—I looked like a falconer!

I picked up dead birds and rabbits on the road and put them in the freezer for meat.

We were set to go.

At least I thought we were.

Everyday, I went to the stall and held out meat on my glove and called her.

For two days she did not come; then, on the third, she did.

She leapt six feet from her perch onto my glove.

In a flashing motion she jerked a piece of meat away and jumped back to her perch.

My lord, can you imagine such?

Our first days started with my ignorance and her fear and hunger.

We taught each other as I fed her.

Imagine this: an evening, I bring her to the house.

I slip one of Jackie's stockings over her.

It holds her tightly, as she lies on my lap and I stroke her with a feather.

She was magnificent!

Her feathers: white on her breast, brown on her back, rust-red on her tail.

Her eyes emotionless, like a snake's.

They saw far off and close up at the same instant.

They were hard...and yet, there was something in them that was lovely.

My only control over her was raw meat: chicken livers, rabbit legs, birds, hog innards.

I took her outside, put her on a fence post with the creance attached to her jesses.

She flew ten feet to me, then twenty, thirty, fifty, then, a hundred.

Are you ready?

I unclipped the creance and walked away.

She was free; with a few flaps of her powerful wings she could soar away into the sky.

But, she came to me.

She came, over and over, as I called her to my glove.

Before setting out, falconers often weigh their birds to be certain they are sharp-set and hungry.

I had no scales; so it was that on this Sunday afternoon, Hawk was not sharp set.

She looked down on me with gorged contempt.

"*HAWK! HAWK! HAWK! HAWK!*"

I yelled as loud as I could yell and plucked as hard as I could pluck.

I pitched the starling on the ground toward her, hoping to excite her.

She turned her head and looked toward the hill, then, at the sky.

I cursed again, worse this time, picked the bird up and began plucking again.

Suddenly, behind me, I heard the crunching of wheels on the road.

The crunching stopped; there was a long silence.

"*Hey feller, whatcha doin?*"

I looked over my left shoulder; there was an old car packed with people.

They could only see me plucking the dead bird.

For a moment, my attention was distracted…"*What?*"

"*Whatcha doin feller?*"

"*What did you say?*"

"*I said, 'Whatcha doin feller?'*"

"*I'm callin my bird.*"

"*Wha'd ya say?*"

"*I'm callin my bird!*"

There was a long silence...a long...long silence.

"Hey feller...that bird of yors is dead."

Lord have mercy, deliver me from my sins.

I did not answer and kept pulling feathers and shaking the starling.

There was another long silence, then the wheel crunching and car went on up the road.

Only a few feathers were left on the bird.

I plucked them off and shook the naked body.

Colonel Benjamin Stainback and Reverend Billy Highfield

Colonel Benjamin Stainback And
Reverend Billy Highfield
On Their Way To The June 3, 1898
Confederate DecorationDay Celebration
In Winchester, Tennessee

"Reverend, they should uv hung that son of a bitch Davis an dug up Calhoun an hung 'im too an then lined up an shot all uv them sons of bitches politicians that got us in that Goddamn war with the Goddamn Yankees, an then we should uv lined up half ir gen'als, with Hood right smack in front, an shot them too...I'm telling ya Reverend, killin six-hundred thousand people just to hold onto a bunch of niggers wus a slop jar full uv shit...an as to State's Rights that's another crock of shit!"

Benjamin Lafayette Stainback,
Confederate Colonel

"The Lawd have mercy Colonel, your sure a booguh man talking thata way, but the good Lawd knows the truth, He knows all about them dark days...you want anothuh drink outah of this jug before I put it back unduh the seat 'way from the sun?...Yes sir Colonel, the Lawd knows, He knows...Get on mules, times awastin, we ain't got all day!"

Reverend Billy Highfield,
Minister and Former Slave

The Colonel

Seventy-two-year-old Confederate Colonel Benjamin Lafayette Stainback was a banty-sized man, only five-foot, five inches tall and getting shorter every year. But he was still tough as a railroad spike and so stern-faced and bad-mouthed that people thought he was taller. He'd been around tough-talking, bad-cursing men since he was eighteen when he went to work for the Nashville, Chattanooga & St. Louis Railway. Then, during the four years he fought with the First Tennessee, the toughness and cursing got worse, and as soon as the war was over he went back among the railroad toughs as an engineer for fifty years. By the time he retired, he could say every curse word the Devil had come up with; and "Goddamn" had become another word like 'the' for him. But he never used any "blackguards," as Miss Lillie called them, when children or women were around. He was as thin as a fence rail. The Colonel's uniform fit him as well as it did when he had first put it on just three weeks before Johnson surrendered him along with the few that remained of the Army of Tennessee over in North Carolina in the Spring of '65.

"Miss Lillie" Jane Wagner, The Colonel's wife of fifty-four years, thought he still looked smart when he was all dressed up in his outfit, especially when he wore his sword that he had not surrendered to the Yankees. She liked to brag to the women at the Estill Springs Baptist Church that he was still the fittest man she had ever seen, "Why, honey, he don't have a slice of pie anywhere on him even though he sho eats like a field hand." And, of course, hearing such bragging, the Church ladies just had to whisper behind their hands to one another about the men who Miss Lillie might have been checking over for pie slices.

She and The Colonel had one child, a boy named Marcus "Mark" Aurelius Stainback. The Colonel had named him. He was so filled with pride to have a son to carry on the Stainback name—a name of no certain origin—that he wanted his given name to be something special. And it was. Whenever anyone would ask, "Where in the world did you come up with that odd name?" red splotches would break out on his neck and he would stare into their eyes like they were fools and after a moment would hiss, "Well, I'll Goddamn tell ye where...as sure as hell my boy's goin to be a great man, so I named him after a great man." Then if they asked him who Marcus Aurelius was he would shake his head and hiss almost as if he was about to strike, "I ain't got time to educate halfwits, so go look it up on your own damn time." Other than himself, Miss Lillie, and the Reverend, there were eleven other people in Franklin County who knew that Marcus Aurelius was one of Rome's greatest emperors: an old Jewish clock repairer, six professors at the University of the South, three lawyers. and one doctor.

Eighteen years after his father named him, Mark was killed on the beautiful morning of October 8, 1862, at the Battle of Perryville. Long years after he died, when Miss Lillie had lady visitors for lunch, at some point she would pick up one of the four framed tin-type photographs of him she had placed around the house and hold it up with his face toward the others and say, "Our Mark would have made such a good daddy if he'd lived, he so loved little children."

The Colonel never got over his son's death. Afterward he never talked about him. He never let anyone see that his heart was broken; he just became more irascible and rough-mouthed. People avoided him when he came to town. Some whispered that he was the one who should have been killed at Perryville instead of his boy, but they were careful who they said it to so it didn't get back to him for he always carried a derringer in his coat pocket and always seemed on the edge of dangerous.

You only had to look at his scarred and purple-splotched hands and muscled forearms to tell that he was old and had worked hard with his body all his life. But his watery eyes were not the eyes of most old people; they could still see as clearly as when he was a boy. They had a haunting, dove-gray color that matched exactly the color of his uniform and were tiny and quick as a mink's, never seeming to rest as they scanned for something far off, or the face of the person standing right in front of him, or the magnificent words of his beloved Shakespeare.

Shakespeare was his Bible. He went to the Bard nightly for wisdom and comfort. There were nights when he was reading a play or sonnet while Miss Lillie was sitting on the other side of the coal-oil lamp reading her Bible that were like heaven. He would look up from his reading and see her looking over her glasses smiling at him, and for a moment his heart would leap and his eyes would mist from loving her so much.

Other than her, there were only a few things in life that gave him much pleasure or rested his unyielding spirit: eating milk gravy mixed with crumbled biscuits—his dessert at every meal; walking with his dog Shep through the fields and woods of his forty-seven acres beside Elk River; reading Shakespeare and memorizing his soliloquies and Sonnets—he was now on number thirty-four—and not having to be around "fools rampant" which included everybody but Miss Lillie and the Reverend.

For thirty years The Colonel and the Reverend had worked together as engineer and fireman in a sometimes burning hot, sometimes freezing cold locomotive cab of the Nashville, Chattanooga & St. Louis Railway. During those years they had grown to totally trust and respect one another and once or twice they had saved each other's life. They knew they were each other's friend though neither had ever said it. They also knew that they were the two most intelligent people they knew with the exception of Miss Lillie whose practical wisdom outranked them both. They were mostly self-taught and, loving books as they did, owned well-stocked libraries of history, philosophy, science, literature, and theology. Their brains forgot nothing they read or heard. In the Reverend's monthly visit to the Stainbacks for supper and conversation, the two of them sprinkled every kind of quotation into their discussions which would grow louder and louder when they were debating fine points of theology or Aristotelian logic and had had too much of Reverend Billy's homemade cider of which The Colonel bought three barrels every year and fermented with molasses. But no matter how much they enjoyed their brilliance, when they were in Miss Lillie's house, her word was law. When they became too loud and too swollen with themselves, she could settle them down with a loud clearing of her throat or with three or four firm words, "Y'all calm down!" or "Y'all, that's enough now!" They would immediately get quiet and, usually, the Reverend would say it was about time for him to be getting back home.

Early on in her marriage to The Colonel, Miss Lillie had realized that she was going to have to keep the bit in "Mr. Stainback's" mouth or someone was going to kill him before he reached thirty—and it might be her. Lillie Jane Wagner was the only creature on earth that The Colonel was scared of.

The Reverend

Except for The Colonel and Miss Lillie, most white people called Reverend Billy Highfield, “Uncle Billy.” He was born a slave on Samuel Highfield’s plantation in Greene County Alabama in 1836. He was a big, light-colored baby and grew into a light-colored, big-muscled man, standing a little over six-foot-three in his broad bare feet that didn’t wear shoes until they were ten years old. Because of his color and high cheekbones, some thought his daddy must have been an Indian.

But it wasn’t his size or appearance that made him special to people when he came to live near Tullahoma; it was his kindness to others, poor or rich, black or white, righteous or sinner. When people needed him, no matter how bad a sinner they were, he went quickly and prayed for God’s help and always left them comforted. The same prayer he prayed for the righteous. Those who knew him well, both black and white, thought he was one of the best people God had put on this earth. He was a happy man with a face that seemed to keep a slight smile as though he was thinking something good. No one could imagine that he ever had a troubled thought. And he loved to laugh, most especially at The Colonel’s colorful condemnations of mankind, though he wished he could make them without saying “Goddamn” so much.

Reverend Billy Highfield was a great preacher. He was known afar for being able to quote all of the Bible and for his sermons on “The Day Christ Died” and “We are All

God's Children." Though he sometimes used words that few in the congregation of the Mt. Zion African Methodist Church understood, they were never troubled since they knew he would never speak a falsehood even with a single strange word. Every Sunday his deep bass voice rolled mercy and forgiveness over them like ocean waves, bringing hope and comfort as did the waters of baptism and the Supper of the Lord.

While he was kind to everyone and was an ordained gospel minister, Billy Highfield made some white men uneasy when they were around him, not so much because of his size but their instinctive recognition that he was far smarter than they were. Only in a whisper did any of them ever say he was an "uppity nigger," and that only when they were certain that the person they were talking to would not pass it along to The Colonel. No man or woman who knew The Colonel wanted those words passed on to him as they knew there was a good possibility of his coming after them with his gun or a knife.

In the fifteenth year of Billy Highfield's life he had been a prime field hand worth over a thousand dollars. However, instead of putting him into the fields, Samuel made him his groom with responsibility for caring for his two fine saddle horses and four brood mares. Three years later he brought him into his own house as his body servant and that same year began to teach Billy to read and write.

Samuel Highfield owned three thousand acres, one hundred and twenty slaves, and the finest library in Green County, Alabama. A year after he was married, his wife Fannie died trying to give birth to a baby boy who was dead inside her. Within one month of Fannie's death, Samuel took her maidservant, a fine-boned woman from East Africa, to his bed. Nine months later Billy was born. Though he was their master and owned them, Samuel loved Mary and Billy; he loved them up to the second he was killed by a Minie ball on the bitter-cold, rainy Friday of December 16, 1864, fighting with the Seventh Alabama Cavalry as part of the rear guard of the destroyed Confederate Army as it began its long retreat southward to Mississippi.

Billy stayed with Samuel all through the war as his body servant. He did not love his father; he obeyed him. Less than ten minutes after he heard that his father had been killed, Billy filled a haversack full of food, hung a bedroll over his shoulder, put on the Major's heavy overcoat, and hid in the woods near Franklin. For two days he stayed there until he was certain all of Hood's Army was gone. Then he began to walk through the mud and ice beside the railroad tracks that led to Tullahoma where his only child Hattie lived. Along with Billy's wife, Liza, Hattie had been sold when she was three to a Tullahoma doctor to pay the large debt Samuel Highfield owed on his land. On the evening of the fourth day, covered with mud and freezing, Billy stepped up onto the platform of the Tullahoma Train Station. An hour later he found his wife and daughter living with an old black woman in a green shack on the east side of the railroad tracks. They had been freed in the summer of 1863 by the Federal Army as it moved south through Franklin County.

On a warm Sunday morning in August 1867, Liza died of "the fever." The day after she was buried in Mt. Zion Cemetery, Billy did what she had been praying for: He confessed that Jesus Christ was his Savior and was baptized. As he would tell his congregation years later, "The day after my Liza went home to be with our Lawd, He reached down with His big hand and lifted my old sinful soul up to Him and washed it whiter than snow...yes, suh, that's what He done for me an that's what He can do fo all sinners who wants to be made clean...praise the Lawd!"

Three months after Liza's death, Billy began working as a fireman for the railroad. On the very first day, when he climbed up into the cab of a locomotive, there was The Colonel. From that day until thirty years later, they worked side by side. When they retired on the same day, The Colonel took Billy's hand in a tight grip and gave him a fine gold watch that he had just received from the President of the NC&StL Railway and said, loud enough for everyone standing near to hear, "Billy, yo're one helluva man. I'm shore gonna miss yore black ass."

Soon after he retired, Billy went to live with Hattie and her husband, John, at their small place a quarter of a mile south of Tullahoma. He began preaching full time, and it was not long before all black people called him Reverend Billy, and so did some whites.

THE WAGON RIDE

Today is a perfect day. Decoration Day, June 3, 1898, and Jefferson Davis's birthday is as near perfect as a day can be. The early morning sun is rising in a pure blue sky; the air is easy to breathe, clean and sweet and filled with the smells of earth and new growth; the road is lined with rail fences and wild rose hedges, red sumac, pink fireweed, and honeysuckle; from the thickets and fields come the callings of thrushes, quail, and meadowlarks; and nearby, to the left of the road where the bank of the Elk River is lined by an old grove of oaks, chestnuts, and maples, a flock of crows rises from their roost cawing to one another as they head to the fields to feed. Almost parallel to the road is the railroad track that runs all the way from St. Louis through Nashville and over the mountains to Chattanooga. In the early morning air the dust from the stirrings of the mules' hoofs and wagon wheels hangs close to the ground, and beyond the fences the fields stretch away in their varied shades of green of the young corn and wheat and cotton and of the pastures where cattle and sheep are grazing. It is a splendid day! Even The Colonel feels it for a moment. Then a train whistle from far behind him breaks the splendor, and he suddenly remembers how much he despises this day.

Every third day of June for ten years, The Colonel and the Reverend have made this trip to Winchester for the celebration. They always left Estill after breakfast at The Colonel's, in the Reverend's farm wagon on which he always puts a fresh coat of green paint and red for the wheels. This morning the Reverend left Tullahoma in the dark. He arrived at the Stainbacks a little before daybreak just as Miss Lillie was taking the biscuits out of the oven. After stuffing themselves with ham and eggs and biscuits and gravy and buttermilk, they climbed up on the wooden wagon seat with the woven basket she had filled with fried peach pies and fried chicken and headed up the lane to the main road where they turned left to Winchester.

The wagon bed is packed with clay jugs of the Reverend's cider which he sells on the square every year and gives one fifth of the money to the Church. And every year The Colonel brings his own jug which now sits between their feet under the wagon seat. They go only a quarter of a mile when he reaches down and lifts it up, pulls the cork and takes two long swigs. When he finishes, he breathes out hard, "Damn, that'll make you strut!" and wipes his lips with his sleeve and hands the jug to the Reverend who takes one short swig and breathes out, "Lawd, Colonel, the way you've stoutin it up is mighty fine!" He shifts his bottom into a more comfortable position and undoes the top button of his shirt in preparation for one of The Colonel's soliloquies, which he knows is forthcoming and which he knows will probably last most of the trip to Winchester.

It begins with a hack and a spit, followed by a loud clearing of the throat. His voice is like a rusty saw. "I'll tell ye one damn thing, Reverend, wearin this itchy wool uniform and walkin in a parade alongside a bunch of farty, ole toothless veterans an listenin to them beat their gums about how we could uv won the Goddamn war if such an such had happened or not happened is worse than bein in the Goddamn war, an then sure as hell they'll start on what a drunk Grant was an what a lunatic Sherman was, an all that stuff is a crock of shit...hellfire an damnation! Grant an Sherman beat our ass! An I betcha one of my jugs aginst three of yours that that damn train from Nashville is gonna unload two or three of those Nancy-boy reporters and one'll come up to me an ask that same old stupid-ass question they always ask, 'Colonel, wouldcha mind telling us why you fought in the war?' That's what they's gonna ask me, why I fought in the Goddamn war! I tell you, Reverend, if I don't shoot im with my derringer I'm gonna scare the shit out of im with my face and voice...'Well, sonny boy, I'll tell ye why I fought in the Goddamn war: cause the Goddamn Yankees were gonna come down here on my land, where my house is, an they were going to upset Miss Lillie, an steal my cows an hogs an whatever else they could lay their thieving hands on...an they were gonna do all that just to free all the niggers, an I'd only owned one of em way back, a no account high-yellar that wasn't worth piss, an when he ran off I almost fell on my knees an thanked the Lord, so I sure as hell wasn't fightin' to keep the niggers...far as I's concerned they could uv had em all free.'" He paused and took a deep breath. "'An one more thing in case you wanta put something in your little piss ant paper bout why I waste my good time dressin up in this monkey suit an comin to these Goddamn things, it's cause I'm a Goddamn hero since I personally shot an kilt eleven Yankees an there's some genteel ladies who love havin a real bonafide hero in the Goddamn parade to march 'round the square, so's I put up with all this damn tomfoolery 'cause they pay me to come an dress up an have my picture made with all the other ole farts.' Then, Reverend, I'm goin to grab hold of his shoulders an squeeze down hard an look straight in his eyes an say, 'Now, does that answer yo stupid-ass question about why I fought in the Goddamn war?'" He stops again. This time his neck is flushed all the way around. He licks his lips, "Good Lord, my spit's all dried up I've run my mouth so much." He reaches down and gets the jug and balances it on his knee and pulls the cork out. "Now, Reverend, you take a lick at the talking for awhile while I get my spit back...tell ye what, I wanta hear how ye come up with those milk-sop names, Kate and Beck, for them mules of yores."

The old preacher is looking straight ahead, his face is set like an amber mask with no emotion. He does not speak for a full minute, then begins, "Colonel Benjamin, you wants to know where those names come from...they comes from a long ways back. Member those dark days, when my peoples were owned by yo peoples...they's the names of two of em who was owned...they's the names of a little brothah an sistah, they was twins, they's had faces like sunlight, smiling an laughin...they's little bitty things but even then yo could see in their eyes they's smart as tacks. They lived right next to us with their mama, so near yo could hear em laughin at night an first thing the next monin they's start all over agin." He stops and wets his lips with his tongue an looks down at his hands holding the reins, he turns them palm up as though looking for something, then continues, "Then one monin the Major calls all us people togethah in the front yard an he walks out of the house onto the porch an looks at us sorta sad like an then he begins talkin an tellin us how he's bout to lose the land an if he don't sell some of us we all gonna be split up an sold away...an ever'body gets real quiet an he says he's done the best he can to sell as few uv us as possible an then he stops talkin an he coughs an then he says he's got to go to town tomorrow an settle up with the bank, an Mr. Haddus–he was the overseer–would let those that's been sold know in the monin an'll help 'em get on they ways with their new masters, an then all the rest of us could rest easy an know they's all be stayin with him. Then he closed his eyes an holds his right hand up high an prays, 'Dear God, watch over these my people. Amen.' An then he turns an walks back in the house an there's not a sound or a movement...it seemed like we were gonna never move agin, an then Big Isaac, the driver, claps his hands loud an shouts, 'Les get on to the fields!'" Now his voice is almost a whisper without the slightest inflection. The longer he talks the fainter it becomes, as though he is going farther and farther away, "So he sold off my Liza an my baby girl, Hattie, an some mo people...an he sold off them two little chillun from their mama...an that's where the mules' names come from, those chillun names be Kate an Beck. I still sees their faces right now while I's talkin, I sees em an hears em cryin for their mama an she be pleadin with em white men that were takin em away." He stops...then,

"An, O my Lawd God, Colonel, I can still sees my Liza an Hattie cryin an lookin at me an I's beggin Mr. Haddus to take me an not take them an...an none of it kept it from happenin, an they just gone...an...an...." There comes another long silence, and then he speaks in a voice The Colonel has never heard. It is cold and hard, and every word is clear, "Even if it was to send me to burn in hell forevah I'd kill any man—even my daddy, if he was to come back—that'd try to make me or my Hattie a slave agin."

The mules' slow, steady plodding has continued all this while, their movement gently rocking the wagon's seat and the bodies of the two silent old men. Both are looking straight ahead toward the distant bridge that will take them over the river and up the slope to the square and the courthouse where the townspeople and the country people have already begun to gather.

The Reverend turns his head and looks at The Colonel, "You know, Colonel, you nevah ask me what it was like bein a slave an I's nevah said a thing til now...folks look at me an they sees a kind-lookin, ole white-haired colahed preacher who likes to help people, an that's pretty much true now, but I hadn't always been this way. A long time ago, before the Lawd an Liza change me, I wants to kill people...wants to kill white people fo what they done to us...I'd wanted to kill you I was so full of hate. Bein a slave is a bad thing, so bad you can't nevah know it, we wadn't mo than a bunch of two-legged animals worth lots uv money...the Major an his wife, they was church goin people who said the blessin at all their meals an always talking bout Jesus an how someday they's goin to heaven, an look at what they did...they's made me hate Jesus an the Lawd God. But all the while I nevah lets on, I's covered it all up, all my sadness an hate, even when they's sold my Liza an Hattie away, I's didn't show nothin cause I's promised her I wouldn't kill someone or do somethin awful an that one day I'd come an find em an we'd be togethah again...An thas what I did...An the Lawd was good to me an forgive my sinful heart an answered my prayers, an so Him and Liza, they's change me an they's teach me to want to be good and to help others an He move my heart to preach His word an help sinners like me to find Him. Colonel, there's many a night I thank Him for you bein my bes friend, 'cause spite the ways you talks an Lawd have mercy how you talks, Miss Lillie wouldn't live with no bad man. All those long years we's workin in that hot cab you was lookin out fo me goin up and down them mountains, and you saves me from dyin fo my time."

He took his straw hat off and raised his tear-streaked face to the sky, "Thank you, Lawd God an Jesus, for giv'n me Colonel Benjamin Lafayette Stainback to be my friend, an, Lawd, lay Yo hand on him an Miss Lillie an give them comfort, an a place with You when they leaves this ole world. Amen!"

When he ended, both were quiet. He put his hat back on, pulled a bandanna from his inside coat pocket and blew his nose and wiped his eyes. Then he smiled and gently slapped the reins, "Get on up there, Kate an Beck, times awastin, we gots money to make."

The Colonel reaches out with his hand and gently pats his old friend's knee.

The mules lift their heads and step out faster. Now, in the warmer air, a little dust rises behind their hoofs and the wheels of the wagon, and from beyond the river comes the first sounds of horns and a drum and the high piercing whistle of the train.

Reverend Billy Highfield's Funeral Oration For Colonel Benjamin Stainback

At the Mt. Zion African Methodist Episcopal Church
In Tullahoma, Tennessee
At 1:00 PM, Saturday, September 9, 1905

Steal away, steal away,
Steal away to Jesus.
Steal away, steal away home,
I hain't got long to stay here.
My Lord he calls me,
He calls me by the thunder,
The trumpet sounds within-a my soul
I hain't got long to stay here.

The closed casket is made of yellow pine, simple, with black wrought-iron handles. There are no flowers on it, no plaque. Inside—his hands crossed on his chest—is a small, gray, wizened man dressed in farm clothes. The clothes are old and tattered by work and wear; the smell of his life is in them, the smell of earth and of war and of perseverance; clothes his wife swore to him she would bury him in, as she swore she would bury him in the Mount Zion Cemetery in Tullahoma. The casket lies on an oak table at the front of the chapel of the white-framed Mt. Zion African Methodist

Episcopal Church. Above the casket, on the stage, behind the pulpit, stands a big, light-colored, white-haired, Negro man. He is old but still straight and strong; his eyes are kind, they glisten a bit with sadness as they look out onto the pew-filled church. His eyes are a comfort to the Negroes who sit before him and, to the few white mourners who do not know him, the old man's kind voice is also comfort in the chapel filled with Negroes. Before them stands a true man of God. For a long moment he looks down on the casket, then, he wets his lips and, in a voice that sounds like God, begins—

"Steal away, steal away, steal away to Jesus...Praise be to Gawd fo the Mount Zion Choir's glorious singin bout our goin home to be hugged by our Jesus.

Glory! Glory! Glory to Gawd in the highest!

Lawd Gawd an Jesus an Holy Spirit, hep me lift up this good man to you in words that give peace to Miss Lillie who the Colonel loved mo than heaben an earth til his final breath. Give me words Lawd to speak glory, mo glory even than tha cry uv a baby jus bawn.

Friends, here befo us lies my dear friend, Colonel Benjamin Stainback: husband, fathah, soldjah, fahmah an chile of Gawd whose spirit has stole away up from us to be with his Savior Jesus Christ.

Today, as we be gathah'd togethah, I wants to talk to you a while bout love: bout Gawd's love, an bout tha love uv Jesus who died fo us, an bout the love uv a man an a woman, an bout the love uv good friends fo one anothah; we talking bout love so powahful Ole Man Death can't lay his cold, bony hand on it...*No suh Ole Death can't kill it! Hear me now—*

Fo Gawd so loved the world that He gave His only begotten son that whosoevah shall believeth on Him shall have evahlastin life....

Thas the promise uv the Lawd...life evahlastin. Praise the Lawd!

Oh Miss Lillie, an all uv my Brothahs an Sistahs in Christ, an all uv you who be friends uv Colonel Stainback, heah the Apostle John's holy words, A new command I give you: Love one anothah. As I've loved you, so you must love one anothah. By this evahone will know you ah my disciples, if you love one anothah.

Next to my sweet Liza an our chillun, I's loved Colonel Benjamin Stainback mo than anyone on this ole earth...Praise Gawd fo bringin us togethah...fo friendship tween a man who'd fought fo the Federacy an a man bawn a slave with hate in him was not somethin meant to be but as we know Gawd's ways be not our ways fo, if they be, I'd nevah have known this good man much less become his friend.

I've know'd the Colonel gettin on to mos forty yeahs. We met two yeahs aftah the wah, the year my Liza died. He was tha engineah an I wus tha fahman fo one uv the ole Nashville, Chattanooga an Saint Louis Railway engins goin tween Nashville an Chattanooga.

Lawd have mercy, let me tell you what happened that first year we togethah. It wus a snowin day in January. We carried a load uv coal ovah to Chattanooga an were headin back home down Sewanee Mountain when, next thing like lightin, we done jump off the tracks an goin straight down the mountain tearin through brush an trees an befo I could shout fo Gawd to save me I feels the Colonel's arms round me like two pieces uv iron an I heah im cussin an shoutin, *Hold on Billy...Hold on!* An we go flyin through tha air an hits tha groun like two sacks uv cawn so hard I thinks we gonna split open an we rolls an rolls down that mountin til I think, Lawd Gawd ain't we nevah gonna stop rollin til we ends up at the bottom uv the earth.

I stand here befo you this very day cause that man lyin there in that pine coffin in his work clothes save me; he saved a po colored man he barely knew. An there, not long befo, he'd been fightin with the Federates an I'd had hate in me.

Listen to me now! Though bad things be in us, Gawd put a good touch uv love in all uv us. I done preach it a thousand times to my flock an I see all ya'll out thah noddin yo heads fo you know them Jesus words I'm bout to speak outta Matthew five, forty-three through forty-five–

Ye have heard that it hath been said, Thou shalt love thy neighbah, an hate thine enemy. But I say unta you, Love yo enemies, bless them that curse you, do good to them that hate you, an pray fo them which spitefully use you, an persecute you; that ye may be the children uv yo Fathah which is in heaben.

Now thah's somthin else needs sayin bout the Colonel, an Miss Lilly can testify to it cause she an I prayed ovah it till our knees give out. Ain;t that right Miss Lillie? What needs sayin is that–the Colonel didn pay much mind to church goin. Cept fo Christmas an Eastah he barely evah set foot cross the church dostep. Though I know he was a believah he said to me once, Billy, you Bible thumpin rascal, if I wus evah to see God's face you know who I'd be seein...it'd be Miss Lillie or you sho as____. Well I won't say the word he said, bein I's standin right heah at the pupit with the good book lyin open on it.

Whooowee! He wus some kind-a stout talkin man. The Lawd have mercy, the words that come outta him on dem trips we made eva yeah togethah in dat ole wagon uv mine, ridin from Estill to Winchestah fo the Decoration Day Celebration. We did'n miss a one cause uv the money. I'd take a load of my cider made from my apple ochawd an, sell it all out. An dem good ladies who put the Celebration on they'd pay the Colonel jus to march with the otha ole Federates since they said he wus the onlyst one that wus a sho nuff hero. When he hear all dat talk bout him bein a hero, it'd set him off like a firecrackah cause he hated dat wah. On the way he'd get to fussin bout the wah an tha genals...fact is he'd get to fussin bout mos anythin til finlly he'd say, Reverend, I done run out uv spit, now you take ovah the talkin fo a spell.

An then come the day, on one uv the trips, I tells him all bout how it wus bein a slave an he don say a word. But when I ends up talkin, I sees tears in his eyes. An, jus bout then, as we starts to cross ova the bridge up ta the gatherin he reaches out an pats me on the knee. Miss Lillie if I hadn't already know'd it befo it wus right then I know'd dat Colonel Stainback had Gawd all in him, no mattah what he'd sometime say.

Praise be to Gawd fo this good man!

Miss Lillie, my ole heart is breakin fo yo hurtin. When my Liza die uv the fevah aftah the wah I thinks how can I go on? But tha Lawd held me up as he will you. In time Gawd'll wipe away the tears from yo eyes; fo I believe that when the times come fo sorrow an cryin, when our love ones leave us an steal away ovah Jordan, even then—mos specially then—our Lawd's there fo us to lean on as He leaned on His Fathah when He hung high up there on that cross.

Hear me preach to you the teachins uv the Lawd! All these thangs are gonna pass away an in the fullness uv time we shall be gathahed togethah again with our love ones. Listen to me now!

Ya'll well know we all made different from one anothah. Look round you. I see it in yo faces. You see it in mine. The Lawd wanted us that way. He mades people not to look like one anothah: so, some uv us be white, some uv us be black, some yellah, some red. An He mades women an men, tall uns an short uns, weak an strong, some fas as a rabbit, some slow as an ole turtle. Yet the Lawd, He loves us all jus like mamas an daddies an granmamas an grandaddies love they's chillun an granchillun even tho each an evah one be different.

Brothahs an Sistahs raise yo eyes upward, fo somewhah up thah in the heabens our brotha Colonel Benjamin Stainback he's now stealin his way home to rest in the arms uv Jesus, an there, close by, waitin to greet him, is his precious boy Mark.

Ah Lawd Gawd on high I sees them through my tears! I's hearin the trumpet sound, loudah an loudah; I's hearin it in my soul, I knows I hain't got long to stay heah. An when I gets there, aftah I hugs an kisses on my Liza, I'm goin ovah to find my friend, the Colonel, an I'm gonna pull him to me an we both gonna laugh an cry cause we ain't got no color on us an he ain't small an I ain't tall—we both jus right!

Please bow yo heads.

Deah Lawd Gawd an Creatah uv the firmaments, an uv all that has been, an all that is, an all that'll evah be. Thou art the one who sent yo son down to die fo us on that ole wooden cross so's we might have a chance uv evahlastin life. Fo that an fo evathin, we love yo Lawd. Now, we, yo chillum, ask that yo receive into yo presence the soul uv this good man, yo child, Colonel Benjamin Stainback...In Jesus Christ's name we pray, Amen.

Brothahs an Sistahs, today, as the Colonel an Miss Lillie wanted it to be, Colonel Stainback goes to rest in the earth near my Liza. Beside him, we leavin a place fo Miss Lillie when it come her time to join him. An, mos likely befo her, I'll join him an my Liza. Fo evah night, I prays on my knees fo my Lawd to call me by the thunder so I won't be long to stay here. Amen.

Death of a Man of God

Reverend Billy Highfield's Words
To The African Methodist Episcopal Church
Tullahoma, Tennessee
Sunday, June 9, 1907

Brothers and Sisters, I heard tell it when I wus bawn I's so big I got stuck comin out uv my mama an tha granny woman like to uv pull my head off gettin me free. But I's made it an so's I stand here taday big as a stack uv hay.

I come inta this world a slave somewhere's roun 1836 on ta ole Major Thaddus Highfield's place down in Greenfield, Alabama. He an his boy Samuel owned three thousand acres an mo'n a hunded uv us slaves; they owned eva hair on my head an eva speck uv flesh on my bones; an would uv owned eva bit inside my head if they could uv got in ta it.

I's Samuel's boy. My mama; she come ova from Africa an worked up in tha big house where Samuel bedded her. When I wus bout eighteen he took me outa tha fields an brought me inta tha big house ta be his body servant. He taught me from tha Bible how ta read an write.

An next thing in years I's a man with a wife name Liza. Lawd God Amighty she was a lovin woman an it wadn't no time til ire little girl, Hattie come ta us like sunshine. An all tha while it was Liza an that Bible wus techin me an I's learnin readin an it began to put a change in me that, aftah a bit, I didn even know wus there.

Then it come about one day, tha ole Major, he calls all us peoples tagethah in tha front yard an he walks out onta tha poch an he looks at us sorta sad like an then begins talkin an tellin bout how they's bout ta lose tha land an if they don't sell some uv us we all gonna be split up an sold away, an eva'body gets real quiet an he says they's done tha best they can ta sell as few uv us as possible an then he stops talkin.

So they's sold off my Liza an, my baby girl, Hattie, an some mo people. An, Oh my Lawd God, I can still sees my Liza an Hattie cryin an lookin at me an I's beggin tha mastahs fo me ta be takin an not them...an none uv it kept it from happenin, an they's just gone...an...an...

Then it came on me so's I wants ta kill people.

You know nobody eva ask me what it wus like bein a slave an I's nevah said a thing til now...folks look at me an they's sees a kind-lookin, ole colahed preachah who likes ta help people, an that's pretty much true now, but I hadn't aways been this way. A long time ago, befo tha Lawd an Liza change me, I wants ta kill people...wants ta kill white peoples fo what they done ta us...I'd wanted to kill em all I's so full uv hate. Bein a slave is a bad thing, so bad you can't nevah know it, we wadn't mo than a bunch of two-legged animals worth lots uv money. When I wus fifteen I wus so big an strong I was a prime field hand worth mo than a thousan dallahs...a thousan dallahs.

Tha ole Major an tha young Majors, an they wives, they wus church goin people who said tha blessin at all their meals an always talkin bout Jesus an how someday they's goin to heaven, an look at what they did...they's made me hate Jesus an tha Lawd God. But all tha while I nevah lets on, I's covered it all up, all my sadness an hate, even when they's sold my Liza an Hattie away, I's didn show nothin cause I's promised her I wouldn kill someone or do somethin awful an that one day I'd come an find em an we'd be tagethah again...an thas what I did...an tha Lawd wus good to me, an fogive my sinful heart an answered my prayahs, an one day, aftah tha wah, it came about that Him an Liza, they's change me an teach me ta want ta be good an ta help othahs an He move my heart ta preach His word ta help sinners like me ta find Him.

But befo then, befo I change, I went off ta tha wah with Major Samuel; we went through some lots uv hell togethah, but I got ta confess it now I ain't eva had a speck uv love fo him. Even when he gets killed comin way from Nashville, all's I's thinking is I's free...I's free...

An then I wents seekin my Liza for I's knows she's been bought by a doctah in a place called Tullahoma. My Lawd it wus some kinda goins ta get there, but I did it.

An tha Gawd uv all glories be praised...fo I finds my Liza an my sweet baby Hattie an we be tagetha again...an Oh my Lawd it wus like I'd died an I's in heaven! Fo three years I's in heaven.

An...Oh my Gawd why...You took er away with tha fever...You took my Liza away...You left me alone scept fo my Hattie...my baby Hattie.

But then, her words come inta me, "Billy, the Lawds doins not ir doins, so we gotta trust that sad times come ta all uv us an thas just that, an so we gotta keep on an do our bes ta help othahs."

So that day, when my Liza went home ta be with ir Lawd He reach down with His big hand an lifted my ole sinful soul up an washed it whiter'n snow...yes suh, thas what He done fo me an thas what He can do fo all sinnahs. An thas what in time, thas what led me ta come a preachah fo tha

Mt. Zion African Methodist Episcopal Church in Tullahoma where now I preached many a year, an many a sermon, an many a weddin an many a funeral.

Whadn't all that long back I preach my deah Colonel Stainback up ta his rewahd. Startin in two yeahs aftah tha wah I wus his fireman on all his engines he drove from Nashville ta Chattanooga. I know'd im mo than foty yeahs an one day he jump with me in his arms from a turnin ova engine an save my life. He wus as tough a man as Gawd evah put on this ole earth but I seen tears in his eyes when I tells im whut it wus like bein a slave. Praise be ta Gawd fo tha Colonel.

I seed in im one uv tha Lawd's great truths, how we all made different. All we have ta do is look round us. Tha Lawd wanted us this way. So He made us not ta look like one anothah. He made some white, some black, some yallah, some red, may even made some spotted or stripped ones; He mades women an men, tall uns an short uns, weak an strong, some fas as a rabbit, some slow as an ole turtle; some got somethin wrong with em, but mos jus right. Yet tha Lawd, says we all his chillum an He loves us all jus like mammas an daddies an granmamas an granddaddies love they's chillum an granchullin, even tho each an evah one be different. I prays on my knees eva night that You, Lawd an Fathah uv all us human kind, ull fogive us fo ir sinful ways an bring us cross tha rivah ta You.

REVEREND DR. JORDAN COOPWOOD'S WORDS
AT REVEREND BILLY HIGHFIELD'S FUNERAL
MT. ZION AFRICAN METHODIST EPISCOPAL CHURCH,
TULLAHOMA, TENNESSEE
SEPTEMBER 10, 1909

Born a slave, our dear brother, Reverend Billy Highfield died a free man of God.

Brothers and Sisters, today we are gathered here together to honor and lift up our dearly departed "Brother Billy," one of God's great soldiers who defended the weak and needy. Longer than most of us can remember he has been an ordained gospel minister of the A.M.E. Church. His words and goodness have spread far and wide leading many souls to God Our Father. In his life he has held our hands and our children's hands through pains and sorrows until we could get beyond them to the other side.

I look out on you and see black and white faces in this filled up sanctuary of folks who love him...most especially his dear daughter, Mrs. Hattie Jackson, and her husband Joe and their five precious children: Matthew, Mark, Luke, John and Hattie Sue. May God dry your tears away and may you always be uplifted by remembering Brother Billy's deep-bass, voice of mercy and forgiveness rolling over you and this congregation, bringing hope and comfort to all of us. He was kind and good to everyone; with always a happy face and smile at the corners of his mouth, as though he was thinking something good about us. When we needed him, no matter what a bad sinner we were he was there to hold us up to God for forgiveness. We will carry him around in our hearts forever.

Let me hear an "Amen" for these words of gospel truth about our Brother Billy.

Lord be praised, your Amens come down on us like cleansing waters of love upon our Brother who lies there before us in his closed coffin. He died as he lived—trying to save others. Yet, like our Lord, he was struck down by hatred. But, as you all know, if he was here to speak today, he would be saying, "Forgive them."

Now, let us lift up our voices to sing his favorite hymns: Swing Low, Sweet Chariot and Steal Away. And when the last note is sung, I want to talk to you awhile more about forgiveness and love, especially toward those who revile and persecute us. For as we all know Reverend Billy would want us to believe on those words of Jesus that guided his life. Don't ever forget them...so join me now in these great going home words, Swing low, sweet chariot, coming for to carry me home...

Tullahoma News. September 10, 1909

Yesterday, Reverend William Highfield was laid to rest in the Mt. Zion Cemetery following services at Mt. Zion African Methodist Episcopal Church where he has been minister for more than thirty years. Three nights ago, "Reverend Billy"; as he was known and loved throughout the county and beyond, was taken from his daughter home, Mrs. Hattie Jackson's home by masked men. The next day, right outside of town, he was found hanging in the woods. His body had been burned. It is reported that this was in retaliation to Reverend Highfield's stopping several white men from injuring Galboa Hanna, a young Negro man from New Orleans, on the streets of Tullahoma. It was claimed Galboa had spoken disrespectfully to a young white woman. Coffee County Sheriff Patrick Vann is conducting the investigation into this terrible crime.

B. J. Tisher

Tullahoma News, September 17, 1909

As reported last week, Reverend William Highfield was laid to rest September 10 in the Mt. Zion Cemetery following services at Mt. Zion African Methodist Episcopal Church where he has been minister for more than thirty years. Coffee County Sheriff Patrick Vann's investigation has, as yet, not identified any suspect, or suspects, who might have committed this terrible crime.

Dear God, You know tha world's going ta hell. If it be thy will, give me tha strength ta help you save it. Amen, B. J. Tisher

B. J. Tisher came out of his mother as ugly as sin: wide-jawed, eyes half-lidded, with a lipless slit of a mouth from where a little red tongue would flicker in and out like sparks when he was angry. As he grew older his anger grew but was seldom seen. He was a short sized man who was convinced he possessed the truth in a world of mendacity created by the words of preachers and lawyers.

His old parents, his wife, and children, loved him to death as did everyone in the Cowan Southern Baptist Church where he'd been an elder for seventeen years and known for the generous doubling of his tithing. Whites in the county, especially those who worked for him at Tisher Coal and Timber Company, looked up to him as the strong voice on the County Court where, as a Squire, he prevented the Negroes from gaining power in the county. Most Negroes feared him. They knew who he really was; when they came on him at work or in town they'd look down, doff their hats and, if he spoke to them they'd say inanities like they were happy—their teeth shining.

The only Negro he'd ever loved was "Aunt Rit"; a tall, rawboned, ebonyed Ethiopian who had been owned by his grandfather. She'd done all his raising while his mother spent her days in bed sipping on her bottle of Laudanum "to quieten my nerves an female cramps." Aunt Rit brought her meals and helped her to the toilet when she was having "one of my faintin spells." The only time his mother left the house was to go into Cowan to see Dr. Fry for more Laudanum or to take "B. J.," as all called her son, to church.

His father was a drunk who spent most of his time gambling and whoring and singing in jail in Memphis.

❧

At times Aunt Rit talked to herself; she'd make strange signs with bird feathers and small, smooth stones; sometimes taking B. J. behind the big house to her cabin in the old, run-down slave quarters where no one could hear them. There, she taught him about evil and hate, how to see them in others, how to drive them away—how to destroy them.

The few Negroes that still lived on the place were scared of her. Among themselves they whispered, "She be a 'Ju Ju Woman' who can conjah away all dem ebil spirits dat fly round an put spells on yuh an fix yuh foevah."

And then it was that one day they were in her cabin alone and no one was anywhere around that she began to say strange words and threw powder on him and then did a thing that made him hate her forever.

A bit of time passed before he set her cabin on fire while she was sleeping.

"Auntie Charlotte Darlin," who'd never gotten over the family losing their land and slaves after "tha wah," would come up from Memphis from time to time to "see if evabody's still alive." Like her sister, B. J.'s mother "Sweetie Pie," Charlotte breathed her breath of interminable vanities into him, "Chile, until we brought tha Dahkies here they were nothin moah than savages an most of em still are. Honey, slavery was God's will, tha Bible teaches it...go look it up, read all tha things about Ham an tha Dahkies. Tha worse thing we eva did down heah was ta lose tha wah an let all of em loose among us. Just you look, now ah days we got Dahkies believen thay's as good as us."

As the years passed Aunt Rit's and Aunt Charlotte's words grew in B. J.'s loneliness and anger and, with the words of the Bible, became the justification for all that he believed and became and did.

B. J. hated Reverend Highfield the first time he saw him face to face on the streets of Tullahoma. Arrogant nigger, he thought, as the Reverend nodded to him with a smile but didn't step off the sidewalk to let him pass. Plus, the Reverend was a good head taller. He hated him even more for this.

And, at that moment, he saw Aunt Rit in the cabin and heard her words and knew he was looking at evil and what he must do. *Tha day's gonna come soon when tha Lord an I'll take care of you.*

THE DEATH OF CHARLIE YARBOROUGH

Tomorrow is just another name for today.
But tomorrow is today.
Yao, tomorrow is today.
The past is never dead. It is not even past.
Grief is better than nothing.

William Faulkner

There may be things stronger than love. I did not know it then. I was too young. My tears felt them but I could not understand.

Death took Charlie Yarbrough away from me forever. I would never see him again. He was thirteen. I was eight. He ran across the street in front of his school bus. A car hit him. That evening my mother told me this in the living room of our house next door to where he lived...where he had lived.

My memory of this, seventy plus years later, comes in tiny pieces; I'm not even certain of the spelling of his name or his age. He could have spelled it Charley Yarbro. He could have been fourteen or fifteen. I could have been six, seven, or eight. Frittering details are not important to the truth of the death of an older boy I admired and worshipped and loved. He was dead. He was gone forever. I would never see him again; never hear his teasing, kind voice; never feel the gentle punch of his fist on my shoulder. I went to my room, got into bed and pulled the cover over my head and cried and wondered, *did he go to heaven, or...or...?* I could not think it and fell asleep.

Those of us who are old know time distorts, reshapes itself; that which was once "real" long years past, even yesterday, can change colors from blue to yellow, green to brown; wispy smells of perfume become chicken frying in an iron skillet; inflections of words, their meanings, can go from love to doubt to anger; what you wanted to exist no longer does.

Though time grinds away at my memory, bits remain. I see myself returning, listening looking for when we were there.

When I was eight, I began to learn that death can take away someone you love and all your tears and all your prayers will not bring them back. That night, as I lay in bed crying and praying, something came into me that I didn't even know was there—my first doubts about God.

With my buddies: Bush, TC, Double M, and Billy Bob, I'd killed thousands of ants and bugs with rocks and matches; we'd knocked sparrows fluttering off limbs with our BB guns. Except for movies and radio and comic books, real death had not touched me, nor them. No one I knew had died; my parents and sisters and grandparents and many, many aunts and uncles were all alive; not one had been killed in the war, or a wreck, heart attack, old age, or from falling off a cliff. I'd not even had a dog die. I'd seen hundreds, probably thousands, of Indians and Japanese and Germans killed in John Wayne movies and Tarzan comic books.

For me, death, "real death" did not exist.

But that changed, not long after Charley was killed death came again with a telephone call to my mother at a nighttime party our family was attending. Her voice breaking, her eyes filled with tears, my mother said, "Billy has been killed in a car wreck." Driving home in the dark, I curled up in the back, hearing my parents whispering in the front, but all I remember is seeing the face of my mother's handsome, older brother and, inside me, a feeling of something that must have been fear. And the next moment I fell asleep.

One after another my grandmothers and grandfathers began to die; then the saddest of all, my lovely dog Dancer, a white Spitz who could dance standing on his back legs died. I dug his grave and buried him in the field behind our house. As each year passed, one after another, aunts and uncles died, and an eighth grade teacher I loved even though he had had me memorize the Book of Acts. On and on death came and took away people I loved.

Finally in 2009 Jackie, my beautiful best friend and wife of fifty-four years, died of cancer and almost to the day, a year later, Adam, our third son was killed in the war in Afghanistan and not long after, my dear, dear, friend JoJo died. Now, at age eighty I wait for who is next.

Many are gone; yet still bits and pieces of them live on in me and others, our memories of them may not be correct; time creates beauty and kindnesses, achievements, meanness and failures beyond what was. Yet, oh yes, yes, some truths remain, some are still alive.

I was baptized in the "Granny White Church of Christ" baptistry in 1948. I was twelve. It made me feel good. I have no memory of it making me better. If it did, it lasted less than a week, for quickly lustful sex was upon me, galloping headlong out of the barn, through my blood with the bit in its frothing mouth.

In 1956, I married my good-good friend, Jackie Burton, a young, southern, "Scarlet O'Hara," slow-voiced beauty: hunter, water skier, funny, intelligent, determined, a good-loving woman of straight-out honesty. Quick as I can type it, we had two sons, and a little later a daughter and then two more sons.

So it was, on a clear-skied, early summer night, not long after our second son was born, while walking on Shy's Hill Road, near our Nashville home, I began to think about God's judgment and heaven and hell, thinking of them as I had been taught in church and school where I'd come to believe, "my Father in heaven" sent sinners who died without forgiveness to fiery hell forever and the few who were "righteous" to be with Him in heaven.

I was being changed reading Greek philosophy and Darwin and Freud. Most importantly, I was learning from the lives of my little psychiatric patients and their parents at Vanderbilt Hospital, where I was a child therapist, who were teaching me to think beyond my certainties about others.

As yet I'd not committed one of the really bad "sins" like: adultery, stealing, killing, cursing God, and on and on. I thought, *well you're probably still safe; you're a pretty good man doing the Lord's work at Vanderbilt Hospital treating mentally ill children.*

At times, my thoughts were depressing and I quit reading and thinking; but, the questions never left me, they always returned and, now and then what seemed an answer.

On that early summer night, I stopped walking, looked up into the sky at stars upon stars shining across the darkness and asked, *No matter what horrors my sons might do in life, could I condemn them to eternal suffering?* And, within the words the answer was, *No!*

At that moment, I knew the best of me was speaking a truth that has never left. With this, came the thought, *if, this is the best part of me speaking, how can God be less?* And there was no answer.

But, before all this—back in my childhood—in my young manhood—dogs and people I loved kept dying. The older I got the quicker they died. My family and friends and fellow Christian believers prayed and prayed and prayed for healing and cures for those they loved and others they didn't even know. Some they prayed for got better, just as many did not and died; for those who died the answer was; "It was the Lord's will." For those who lived the answer was, "It was the Lord's will." As those I knew died and disappeared, "the Lord's will" slowly began to die with them.

As it slowly came to me that *love and religion and belief and prayer are not enough*, I began to step away from God

From February 1963 to June 1968, I kept an irregular journal of Jackie's life and mine with our five children during our twenty years living in a steep, forested hollow of sixty acres in a remote, hilly area of Williamson County. After 1968 the thirty-three recordings had long breaks with

the last one in August 1986 after we'd moved back to Nashville.

The following excerpts from the journal—exactly as written—can be found in the complete journal in my book, *Come Sit With Me* and in the *2013 Williamson County Historical Society Journal.* The selected excerpts present some of the continuing changes in my beliefs.

Introduction...[Shortly before Christmas 1962, Jackie and I moved with our first three children from Nashville] to a rural, almost wilderness area [in Williamson County], filled with all kinds of wild animals and unusual people. Within a mile-radius of our house, which was surrounded by heavily wooded hills, hollows and fields, lived a bootlegger, a moonshiner, a shell-shocked veteran of WWI, a lady of ill fame, a black farmer who owned a rooster that laid eggs, a woman who shot her husband to death, a few mentally ill and retarded folks, and a yeoman farmer and his sons who became life-long friends with our family. No one was boring.

Now, [in 2012], I am seventy-five; my words may have inaccuracies, or flat-out untruths, as I am calling on memories of times long past. Also, Jackie would correct me from time to time when I stretched the truth in telling something. Likely she was right; on the other hand, I believe facts can sometimes stand in the way of creating a good story. Now to the journal...

Feb. 1, 1963. Today my grandmother, my mother's mother, died. She was eighty-nine and her face even in death showed her goodness. And so one generation departs to make room for the next and we take another step toward our final destiny. I was the last to see her alive and knowing that she would be gone before the sun came up I smoothed her hair down gently...I loved her but to be truthful my grief was small as in so many ways she was already dead these last years. Her mind was childish and she lived in days of before. I know she was proud of me and because of this and her own example I must meet her great expectations...

Feb. 20, 1963. All men seem in some way to desire immortality whether in a life hereafter, their children, or through the monuments of their lives. I am not sure of the first, we pass quickly from the minds of our own seed (unless they can benefit from their remembrance) and the elements of time eat away the faces and souls of a few. Could the writing of this journal be an attempt at that first golden ring? (*Added years later–"for the most part this is ostentatious claptrap, attempting to sound like Thoreau who I've loved from then 'til now."*)...

Aug. 1-2, 1964. Spent both days back in the hills on horseback searching for a downed plane. [Got] lost Saturday for 3 hrs. but finally found way to Mr. Joe Dickinson's...On the second [day] with large body of horseman got pitched on my head when Lady tripped over an obscured fence. Called in at 2:30 to announce plane wreck found & passengers (Jim Reeves & ?) discovered near Franklin Rd. Both men dead. My rear has two large sores & hurts like blazes...

Feb. 10, 1969. My first published poem Leningrad 1941-1942 comes out this month in Soviet Life mag. The editor of S.L. is presently first secretary to the Soviet Embassy in Wash. D. C. [I asked Jackie if she would defect with me to Russia since they appreciated my writing more than America. She didn't laugh.]

Writing for me is very hard as I have done enough reading to realize my own poverty such as the first of this journ. Which smacks of 17th Cent. England. I must have started it on a romantic binge. Yet I know the real basis—I don't want to completely & totally die doubting immortality I still want to be remembered—at least for a while by my family.

Jackie sometimes tells me I don't need her or anyone as much as she and others need people—I could get along even if some calamity took them all away. This was not said as a complaint, nor in anger, only as an observation of fact. Maybe so for this is the basis of the B.B. [My poem, The Black Boar] Within my thoughts I am always muddling around with my own isolation & separateness. Yet how I do enjoy being with & talking with friends. But do I really need them for themselves?

Sept. 9, 1969. All back in school, thank goodness for Jackie. I continue to concern myself with some basic differences in my beliefs & those taught at Lipscomb i.e. the interpretation of man's blunders & faults resulting from sin (Lips.) or as W. Faulkner said, " man ain't got any morals, he just does what he's able." This later is not as pessimistic as it appears on hearing since man is capable of doing more—rising above himself—through the help of other men as is learned in all close relationships of love. Maybe the children will not come out so confused, rather if given the opportunity they can select the best of both sides to develop their own individual beliefs, for in truth the religiously convicted people tho sometimes doing little mean things [and sometimes helping evil i.e. slavery and genocide against Jews] & still are those most deeply concerned with helping others. Seldom does it seem that the man carrying the great banner & marching for the "general good of man" give the attention which is his responsibility, to those closest to him. Extremists are all alike—standing back to back, so close they cannot see they are touching rather than opposite extremes. Am reading *The Man From Monticello* & *Men in Groups*.

Last night when I was 1 hr. late arriving home Lynch with his usual humerous ways commented, "Well, I guess he's out gambling again."

Sept. 9, 1986. In bed sick 4 days, detached, no interest. Am losing a sense of caring about my work [Dir. Columbia Area Mental Health Center], friends, family. The exception is Jackie—I feel more dependent on her as my self assurance diminishes. My self centeredness is unhealthy & boring & yet outward goals & interests don't last. *[The final entry.]*

On May 25, 2009, Jackie died of cancer in our library looking out onto her garden.

On May 6, 2010, Adam, our third son, was killed: by a roadside bomb in Afghanistan.

Neither love nor prayer kept them alive.

Like Charlie they disappeared except for their remains in the hearts of those of us who loved them and...

...In time, we will all disappear with them.

Clocks slay time...
time is dead as long as it
is being clicked off by little wheels;
only when the clock stops
does time come to life.

Faulkner

And now, toward the end of my life, as I near my own death, I know there is nothing greater than my love for Jackie.

www.ingramcontent.com/pod-product-compliance
Lightning Source LLC
Chambersburg PA
CBHW020552310726
48979CB00008B/1182/J